Way Ward
Life
_R

Ron
Young

DORRANCE Publishing Corporation

c.

WAYWARD LIFE

BY AUTHOR RON YOUNG©

DORRANCE PUBLISHING CO., INC.

PITTSBURGH, PENNSYLVANIA 15222

Way Ward Life

by

Ron Young ©

DORRANCE PUBLISHING CO., INC.
PITTSBURGH, PENNSYLVANIA 15222

The contents of this work, including, but not limited to, the accuracy of events, people, and places depicted; opinions expressed; permission to use previously published materials included; and any advice given or actions advocated are solely the responsibility of the author, who assumes all liability for said work and indemnifies the publisher against any claims stemming from publication of the work.

Dorrance Publishing Co., Inc.
701 Smithfield Street
Pittsburgh, PA 15222
Visit our website at www.dorrancebookstore.com

ISBN 10: 0692448160
ISBN 13: 978-0692448168

Table of Contents

PREFACE

Everybody needs a getaway from the normal mundane lifestyle of routine work and happenstance. They need an outlet that leads the imagination into a different time-period. A time period that represents the difference in the lifestyle between now and the 1800's, understanding that a hundred years ago people lived much simpler lives that had various outcomes, and conclusions that represented how hard work adds to success.

We all like to recall our childhood memories and the way things used to be when we were growing up. Listening to our grandparents ramble on endlessly about how we have it easier and how they had it harder growing up than what we have it now. *Wayward Life* is a story about a boy growing up on a Tennessee farm with his family in the late 1800's. This story whispers the sound of Civil War and the beginning of the industrial revolution that made America such a great nation.

The main character, Christopher, explains the hardships and uncertainty of the small farmer. The small farming communities that emerged during the Civil War have relevance as to keeping the country going during a time of war. Christopher tells a story about what hard work ethic, good integrity, and study can do for him and his family living on an 1800 farm. Some of which *Wayward Life* displays to the reader is how the family interacts and pulls together to accomplish tasks that are invited into their day-to-day lives. *Wayward Life* also has a child's like playfulness between friends and family that most often creates a tight bond between family siblings and friends. Simplicity is the key; thus, passing knowledge from one generation to another, Christopher and his family (the Smiths) survives our changing America during a time of war and industrial revolution.

This is a fun-loving book about a boy named Christopher Smith who tells his story about the South during the late 1800's. Christopher lives on a farm located in Knoxville, Tennessee, owned by his father, Henry Smith and his mother, Rebecca Smith. His family pulls together to get the farm work done; when they are not working on chores, Christopher, his brothers, sisters, and friends find time to play. This story goes in depth about growing up on a farm and the trials that present themselves while working on a farm. Many tasks are part of the everyday life of Christopher and his family, such as selling at the market, building houses, and finding new means of transportation that is, trains, and bicycles.

They have an uncle, Nick Smith, who lives in Nashville, where they like to visit. As Christopher stays at Uncle Nick's house and plays with his cousins, he notices that keeping close to family is important. Christopher finds himself in a world of war and peace at the same time, holding on to family and school values in an uncertain South that is in the midst of abolishing slavery.

Thanks

A special thanks to my family and friends, hope everyone enjoys reading Way Ward Life a book that explains life and how it can change.

~Chapter 1~
The Way Life Is Here

The Way Life Is Here

Farm life can be boring compared to big city life. We wake up at 4:00 am in the morning to start eating breakfast that Mom cooked. By 4:30 am, it is off to the morning chores getting the cutler ready to plow the main crop. This can be a hassle, especially for children. We have to put the harnesses on the two pulling horses, pull back the steer, and clip it to the holster. Thus, daily chores consist of milking cows, cleaning the chicken coop, washing the pail buckets, making sure the horses' troughs are full, and getting much of the other tasks done before Dad and my older brother, Chipper, get back from walking over the fields. It may sound like I do all of this work by myself, but my brothers and sisters help out, too.

If we get our chores done early, we have plenty of time to play. I mostly like to play on the farm; you have this and that are dangerous according to mom. Playing in the open field is the most fun. Inviting a couple of friends over and running through cornfields never gets boring. You may have a little itch every once in a while, but it will go away.

My dad, a nice man, he is tall, stalky, and dark. Dad looks like a person that always stays out in the sun.

His height is about 6'9" and he looks stern. Scratching on his curled up Texas gunman mustache being mindful of time; he likes to make sure that all of the farm work is completed by midafternoon.

It is not very bad if we get all of our chores done in the morning time. This leaves us plenty of time for, as our schoolteacher, Miss Parity, calls it, "grammar".

Thinking about the word, "grammar", gives me a vision of a person walking with a book on top their head or a child with a dunce hat on, sitting in the corner of a classroom.

I only have to go to school three days a week but when my Mom or Dad says, "it is time for your studies," we all stop what we are doing, look around in a circle, then pout, and finally walking inside to sit around the fireplace readying ourselves to read some books.

Miss Parity tells us to choose a book from the old bookshelf at the rear of the classroom at the beginning of every week. Then she writes down the name of the book and assigns a book report due by the end of the week or the beginning of the following week. Depending on how gracious Miss Parity feels she will allot more or less time to complete the book report. For the most part, we do not even finish reading the book by the end of the week.

Carrying a book everywhere you go, only produced missing books, Mom and Dad had this problem with Chip. They only allowed us to read books in the study or gathering room and when I had gotten done with the book, I was reading, Mom would tell me to put the book on the bookshelf until school. The next morning, Chaney, Susan, and I would take our books and put them inside our big rainbow-colored book strap before walking to school. Every Friday, we often told the class what we had read. The first half of chapter two of *Moby Dick* was what I did my report on this time around. My report went something like this:

"Herman Melville, is the author of the book, *Moby Dick*, and Ishmael, the main character of this novel, went out sailing with some of his friends". "Ishmael hangs at a bar in Nantucket, where a man named Lazarus sits on the curb in front of the establishment, which they say is a dive". "The title of the second chapter of Moby Dick is Carpetbagger", this is all I have written down and I expect the class will ask questions and anyone who has read the book before will help me answer those questions.

Every Friday after show and tell, everyone in class gets a new book; we do the same process every week. I really do not understand how effective this way of schooling is, but Miss Parity made it clear that she did not want any, "gibberish talk in her school-house." Math is the other subject we have to study. I hate math with a passion, it is something that I am just not good at. Most of the class knows that farm work is a dozen of this and 1 or 2- gallons of that, all we have to know is how much a bucket can hold 1-gallon bucket or 2-gallon bucket, the size of the milk churn, which are, 5-gallon and 10-gallon, and how many eggs to place in a box you know 12, 24, or 48, 1 dozen, 2 dozen, or 4 dozen.

Everything else only stacked, my father would call out "4 feet bundles only!" and that is how high it would be when the men finished stacking. Every day, I have to count to 100, write it in the gray ledger book, and then write my ABC's under neither each count. My brother Chaney says, "This type of schooling keeps us sharper than the other children who do not attend school." Chaney likes to use his schooling to count playing cards. School really benefits Chaney. It gives him an opportunity to show off his trickery skills. "It is just like magic: You have a bad hand and still the pot disappears." This is the way Chaney is; he always looks for a way to deal someone out of belongings.

Dad believes in schooling, his father had school and he had schooling. There is no way I can get out of it. Grandpa always said, "A dumb apple falls first." When I asked Mom what Granddad meant, she just smiled and laughed. All of us have to calculate all the way up to 100 using addition and subtraction problems, you know, 4+4=8 type stuff. We never multiplied much, that is for college students. Our School House is a one-room schoolhouse with red outer walls, a bell on the top, [like a church] with two windows on each side. The schoolhouse has front and rear doors with windows on the left and right of each door. A two-step foyer leads you inside from the front of the schoolhouse. The front is where the oak tree is, shading the sunlight with its big shadow, which is the place my friends and I mostly hang out. We run around the big oak tree, playing chase and other games. A swing sits off the tree with a large bench that can hold three children at a time. When we finish playing on it, we latch the swing to the side of the tree, with a big tug rope. A dip pit underneath the tree where the old swing used to be and a pile of dirt under the new swing makes it seem like you are going up and down while running around the tree thus making you very dizzy.

The rear entrance has a little ramp that runs us directly into the rear door. We sit all grades from front to rear; there are about forty children in all. You could say the schoolhouse is very well ventilated because when winter comes through, it gets very cold inside. We wear long underwear and extra clothing to protect ourselves against the cold. By December of last year, Mom made us these huge sweaters to wear to school; we called them our winter sweaters. I only liked to walk to school in this big sweater because they are so full of cotton that the sweater is itchy. Once I got to class, I would hang my cover and jacket at the entrance, remove the sweater that made me look like a little sheep, then sit on the sweater, which makes me as tall as the older children.

The schoolhouse has a fireplace on the left hand side between the two windows, but even when the fire is going it is still cold. Before the class day starts, the girls sweep the floor and dust, while the boys collected up fetch and sticks from outside to keep the schoolhouse clean. "Cleanliness is next to godliness," Miss Parity would say.

I go to school every other day. Poly is yet too young to go to school so she stays home with Mom. Chaney and Susan are both around the same age, fourteen and thirteen; both of them are getting ready to graduate school. My older brother, Chip, did not have to go to school because he had already graduated. Father and he go straight out to the fields every morning and work the fields with the people they called *hands*.

A *hand* is a worker that Dad or Chipper hires in town to help with the fields. Mr. Riley is a regular, he is no hand. Mr. Riley is an old black man that lives down the street, he and my Dad have been good friends for a good long time. When the McBright's left to head South, they left some of their farmland to Mr. Riley, but only enough to eat off of and have a garden sale or two. The McBright's must of befriended Mr. Riley kindly to leave him that little something to live off of. The McBright dwelling is located two farms down from us in Knox, Tennessee. The couple has a farm about the same size as ours that they like to grow cotton on. My brother, Chip, called it tumbleweed because it is one of the easiest crops to grow and sell. The climate is a little too dry for cotton in Tennessee cotton is a crop made more for Mississippi. We did not have many cotton growers in Tennessee because of the climate. It just gets too dry in Tennessee to grow cotton.

The McBright's left because they had a bad year; after not making the sales, they were fed up with the drastic change in the climate. One year it was scorching hot in the summer time and freezing cold with snow in the wintertime; the next year, we had a cool summer and no wintery weather at all. The McBright's did not like the unstable temperature change. The rain differs here with unstable humidity; it really becomes a mess for the farmers who plant very large fields with wheat and barley with no helpers. When the McBright's decided to finally leave, Mr. Riley stayed behind. My guess is that the McBright's no longer wanted to use him on their farm, especially with the Civil War going on. As the fight gets fierce, using slaves for help causes a lot of trouble in this undecided Tennessee south. I have even heard of a man in East Tennessee who kicked his wife out because she was for the Confederate Army. The hotels and railroad companies have stopped using Orientals for local work. Now, they have to pay and service pays well.

The McBright's liked my father so they asked him to watch after Mr. Riley because Mr. Riley worked hard and was a fair man, the Mcbright's knew it. They asked Dad and Mom to make sure Mr. Riley did well. Later after the McBright's left, Mr. Riley married a young Indian woman in town, she is a peaceful soul and keeps to herself. He married a little squall that lived in town. She helps work the market area every weekend. Mr. Riley's wife does not actually speak much, I think she is a mute; the word around town is that she ran into Dunkin and Kid and they cut her tong out. I do not know if all of what is passed around town is true, but the fact of the matter is Mr. and Mrs. Riley seemed to make a good couple.

Dad taught us to respect other people. Dad said, "You are going to have to use your head one way or another rather have you study than ram it through a door," which my brother Chipper likes to do every once in a while any of the way.

I have five siblings that live with us, my brother Chaney the second to the oldest, Chipper, my oldest brother, Myself Chris. I'm only nine. The three C's is what Mom came up with, my oldest sister, Susan, who is the third oldest and my little sister, Poly, who is the youngest. We like to play in the side yard of the old decked house in Knox, Tennessee, on the side by the big red barn house.

My Dad's friends live down the street. Every weekend, they walk or ride their horses down the hill to talk new ideas with my father. Big ideas because farmers are always looking for business opportunities, weather it is in the logging industry or the train industry, or even local merchandising, selling of goods to the new market that they had built in town or just trying to make farm life easier. They liked to come up with new crazy ideas for irrigation and water conservation for building fields. They have been planning to buy the old lumber mill plant from Boones and make it a butcher shop so the local farmers would not have to auction cows in town. The farmers could then sell their own beef and have the town people travel to the country and buy beef. These were good ideas that my father and his friends sat for hours and talked about every week. The town's farmers would post something new in the local newspaper flyer. They never acted on their ideas; this type of news keeps our little town going.

We called it bucky talk, all it was is poppy kaush people talked about, and the townspeople had nothing but a good time while doing it.

Every week, my father's friends would switch the meetinghouse that they gathered at. Every once in a while, Dad would take one of us children over to his friend's house, it always worked well with boring conversations or bad subject matter, both of which my Father did not like. He could then tell the neighbors, "My son or daughter must be tired", "I'll go ahead and take them on home now". The other men Mr. Preston, Mr. Woods, Mr. Farrow, and everyone else that was invited started to bring their children too; it gave us a time away from school to play with friends that honestly live too far away, to play with every day. I get to see friends that live five and six hills away every time we go to one of my father's meetings. We get to have fun when all the neighbors get together.

Even if they are playing cards, then most of the time Dad will bring Chaney along, all of them old men called Chaney a cheat, that is the term Mr. Woods uses when someone asks his son about a bad hand. They argue every once in a while but it seems my father has a skill for debating at the card table. Then they calm down, laughing at each other because they all know that yelling at one another is not the way to play cards.

Chip can hold his own in cards, especially poker, Chip always comes up with an excuse not to play. He said, "Why would I want to lose my belongings to card sharks when I have a new guitar to buy".

Chip had his own thing going on, he liked to play the guitar and he played it well. Chip gave a square dance or two with the barbershop folk in town. I could see Chip at nightfall sneaking out the door with Susan and Chaney to play in town, then the horse wagon would screech and off they went with the four horses and behind them a dust cloud that followed. Occasionally, Mom and Dad went to see Chip play, Mr. Riley and his wife would come over to house sit my little sister Poly and myself, while my parents are away.

Every time they would come over to house to sit, Mr. Riley's wife would bring a gift. My father told him, "Hey you are part of the family, you do not have to bring anything", but Riley's wife insisted on bringing something for their kindness to her husband. She was a beautiful Indian woman with long gleaming hair and the smile to match it. Mr. Riley was much older than she or her being an Indian, you could not tell her age.

~Chapter 2~
My Father, Mr. Henry

My Father, Mr. Henry

Understanding that dads will be dads, my father who never wants to be called by his last name, I guess it means that he is getting older or something, I even call him Mr. Henry and I am his son. You know, he is my father and all. I never disrespect his wishes. His full name is Henry Smith but everyone calls him Mr. Henry. You can tell him something until you are blue in the face, if it is not in front of him written on paper, you will get a delayed response, you may get something more like a so what do you want me to do about this! and then a grin. After that, he takes a cool sweep with his left foot, grabs his chin, and pulls down on his hat. While pulling on his hat, he pulls out on his suspenders before giving back an answer. "Well, go on out and fetch some water while I deal with this", Dad would tell Chip or Chaney. He sends you away, when you get back, the problem is solved.

I have always thought of my father as being a tough guy. He has the gun fighter look, black sweeping hair swept from right to left, with a half beard and a curly mustache that has been in the family tree longer than the tree has been planted. All of the Smiths like to show their large mustache off. I even see Chaney trying to grow one but his is just a little fur patch that he combs every once in a while to seem dignified. Chip, my oldest brother, just does not look good with our family mustache. His hair is blond, it will not show up right because you see through the hair on his face and it is straggly looking like a possum hanging from a tree in midsummer. Chip has what Mom calls her sweepee face, the type of face that could not lie to save itself.

See Chip is what we call a good smiler. He throws one out every once in a while and ends up with the girls because of it. Chaney has the poker face he hides his emotion well; too many women are attracted to his sneaky look. They always ask about Chaney because he looks like a bad guy. My father, a sharecropper from Pennsylvania, spent most of his life on an old farm located in Hershey, Pennsylvania, that my Grandpa and Grandma owned. They owned the farm and operated it. Granddad finally sold out after Ma died. He sold it to a big business when they wanted to build a plant and needed space to locate workers. Granddad gave my Father and Mom the old title deed to our farmland located in Knox, Tennessee. This is where we reside now.

Granddad went on to work doing sales in New York for Macy's. and my father and Uncle Nick moved to grand old Tennessee. They said this state has some class because it has an Opera House and a tug barge everything you need to run a major business. When things go, wrong, Dad and Mom are the first one to know about it. Dad likes to be in charge of every situation and he uses Mom as the brain. Dad would say that left hand of mine makes me look good. Mom kept the farm going by making necessities that you could not get anywhere else. Some of the stuff she made included gloves, bonnets for the girls, and Mom repaired shoes. Well, Mom repairs them until we can get to Uncle Nick's house. Uncle Nick is a cobbler, so he does a better job. Uncle Nick usually gives us a free pair or two for working at his shop in Nashville.

Mom is part of Dad as Dad is to himself. The two do just about everything together. When you see one, you usually see the other they go hand in hand like a door and a doorknob, they make sense. The farm is the other part of Dad's life that makes him the mighty man. He likes to hang outside on the farm all day long, figuring out where to move this and how to fill that, smoking his pipe, and walking along the back trails to get to where he wants to go. Dad hires the hands and they work all day, especially during harvesting season, which is May 1st, Jun 15th, July 6th, August 21st, September 15th, October 1st, October 15th, November 1st , and December 5th. During the winter, we only grow herbs and spices and anything you can grow underneath a tent to protect the crop from the frost.

My father is generous to the hands. He gives them all a fair amount of the wages 2.50 cent a day and 1 sack of food per day is enough to keep the family feed and buy some nice knick knacks along the way. As you could guess, too many people in town want to work for my Father. The work is long, hard, and tedious. Most of the men he hires are middle-aged men with families to support. Father has always had a soft spot for a man with wife and children, he said, "It helps if a man can provide for his family." Dad never misses a Sunday in the hot Knox Chapel. He is there every weekend whether he is tired, sick, or not. We are right beside him listening to Reverend Pickard telling us how much we have sinned in the last week. Religion is important to my Father he prayed before every meal and did not eat a lick without someone to share it with.

My father loves to read the newspaper. He would read the same one newspaper all week long. The only place you can get a newspaper is in town. The Knoxville Journal is the only newspaper around. Dad picks one up every Saturday while we work at the market. As we sell fruit and Mom's marmalades, he sneaks off just long enough to spend his five cents on a fresh newspaper. Knoxville Tennessee is a calm area with a small population of only about eighteen thousand people that actually live in the area. Wayne County has more farmers than Knox. If you wanted well-grown fruits and vegetables, you would go to Knox, if you wanted a large amount of farmland, you would move to Wayne County, and if you wanted to lumber and log, you would go to Chattanooga. For lodging and hunting, you would go to Yosemite Park. It is ran and owned by no other than Wild Yosemite Sam. His family governs the whole hunting area at the park. No one gets in without first meeting Yosemite Sam, if he does not like your type, you might as well get your stuff packing.

We live in Knox County off of Orchard Drive, at the end comes my house. We have sycamore trees growing in groves outside. It is an art sapping this type of tree; the Indians make long pipe steams with a sharp end; with a pipe nasal at the other side that is sanded by flint rock tied together with a little twine to keep the opposite end the nozzle on. My dad liked to smoke out of the sycamore cipher or sapper that is what the locals call it. They say a long pipe makes a man look important. The longer the pipe is, the smarter the man looked. Take, for instance, General Jackson and his pipe, it was long enough for him to push charred apple into and it had a narrow shaft just like my Dad's pipe. A pipe with the type of shaft that a man could look down and see his own smoke ring coming out of it is what most men liked to show off in the South. Generals had these types of pipes and they put them in their amour on a boat stand this keeps the pipe dry, the boat stand was actually used for drying tobacco leafs; everyone in the South, knew it did a better for pipe display.

Our pipes might seem small compared to the type the Indians liked to smoke off of because Indians liked to smoke gigantic peace pipes. All night long, you see them along the short trails of the Blue Ridge Mountains and along the way to North Carolina, the path called the "Old Wheat Way Trail", smoke rising from no man's land. Most everywhere, now a day's men have decided that they like to act dignified, well mannered, accustomed to Southern hospitality. This keeps troubles away. The types of trails that Indians live on are located along the Appellation Mountains; these winey roads leads to the North through foothills. The Indians like to bargain with the travelers and steal from the lone riders that pass through. Stories of Indians run rampant
around these parts, the one I remember was told by Grandpa. He told us about Chief Eagle Spear when the Unami Indian Tribe held my Great Uncle Stein by the New Jersey Delaware border while he was working in a little missionary, town called Chandelier. Chief Eagle Spear surrounded the town. This town was newly built. They had lived in it for a year or two. The Indians said they owned the land and were willing to fight for it. My Grandpa got his shoot and his rock thrower, that is what they called the old hand gun, and went to New Jersey with his four brothers. His brothers included Great Uncles Michael Smith, Jack Smith, David Smith, Eric Theodore Smith, and a couple of the townsmen in Hershey, Pennsylvania. Some of the McDonalds and McDowell's also came

out to help my Great Uncle Stein with his Indian dilemma.

My Great Uncle Stein sent two messengers out one to my Grandfather in Hershey, Pennsylvania, and another to William Sprahawk in Brighten Massachusetts. William Sprahawk and my Grandfather met up around Cape May. After meeting, they came up with the plan of all plans. The small brigade would take a couple of horses behind the Indians and chase the Indians out of the area. After riding into the back forest, the men got into what is called a "horse fight," that is how my Grandpa explained it. A horse fight is when you are chasing and firing at the same time. Surrounding the Indians from all sides, William Sprahawk's brigade put up a good fight that lasted two days. It seemed the Unami Indians were not going to yield that is one thing about Indians they never give up. When the Indians finally gave in and started to move back, William Sprahawk led a chase to the New Jersey side of the Delaware Bay that scattered the Unami. When the Unami re-gathered, the Governor at the time, Williamson of New Jersey, offered them another land just north of the border. They latter relocated Chief Eagle Spear to upper New York near Alfred and the Unami tribe disappeared.

Tennessee, honestly, is no place for setters. If you have a do nothing, it is not in Knoxville; we always have work, whether you are helping a neighbor or someone else. I know about hard work because it happened to my brother, Chaney; when he had a do nothing to do attitude and did not want to work on the farm, Dad sent him off. Dad sent Chaney to work with the Foresters, Uncle Samuelson's family, for the whole summer, and when Chaney came back, he was happy to do as much work on the farm as he could. Chaney would say, "Look, move out the way short stuff, this is easy work compared to logging and tree removal in upper Virginia", Chaney stayed with Uncle Samuelson in Alexandria, Virginia, yawing mules to pull logs in the summer heat all summer long. It seemed that people that do not want to work in Tennessee got out sourced to somewhere else worse than where they had started.

I remember Dad outsourcing Chip's leadership skills to the church orphanage. Chip said, "They did more work in one hour than what we did on our farm in a whole day", "All that moving beds and cleaning took most of the orphanage's day up." Then Chip told me about the two decks of white marble floor that had to stay white and when Preacher Bryant came out to inspect the orphanage he traveled all the way from Alcona Michigan. Chip's words exactly, "Just be glade for what you have because it may just go away in a flash." Dad went out to meet Preacher Bryant. Preacher Bryant was somewhat of a legend in the New United States. No one ran more missionaries than Milton Bryant. He saved children's lives that were abandoned by their parents, parents who had died in the war or by any other incident. The Michigan Prime Ministry sent Preacher Emery Bissel to help Preacher Bryant. They ran the best orphanages in the better-known U.S. The Knox Tennessee orphanage owner, Father McEgret, used to call Preacher Bryant acting Pope of the North or 13th Pope because he relayed messages from Pope Pius XII of Rome.

Hard work belonged to Tennessee, and nothing came easy. Old Blue our hound dog, if he could speak; of all of the floods and bad irrigation canals Dad, Chip, and Chaney had fixed, he would tell you it made for way too much work for the old dog to watch. Blue would step out on the porch with a tail wag like he was the one doing the work, then lie down in your work area until you tell him to get, get on out of here old dog, your making bad work.

People are generally nice in our area. They like the Southern life sitting and watching the grass grow is just not our style, if there is an event going on we are there helping it out and making it the best event it can possibly be. For Dad, going to the Gallery when it opens every year, and getting a farmer's spot at the gallery is a joy. He likes to show off our new lifts and field equipment that replaced our old equipment on the farm and the Farmers Gallery is place to do it.

Once every year, we have a display area for new equipment and horticulture examples at the Gallery Show. We set up displays such as new ways to irrigate water, piping pumps, and have demonstrations on how to make sprayers for farm fields. This year, my father is planning on making a cart track system for our farm. He has not yet started putting it together, but Dad is going to display it at the next Farmers' Convention. This is the type of stuff that we like to do in this town. A lazy man makes nothing happen, so your best bet is to be on your P's and Q's.

My Father has a system about him. It is my way or nothing. He ate three times a day exactly at the same time you are supposed to eat. Dad ate once early in the morning, once at midday, and once at dinner. We all get too hungry to wait for mealtime. You can see us children snaking on a piece of fruit from the orchard because we are plumb tired and need something to tide us over from the summer heat. Waiting on a meal makes you too hungry, especially when working around the farm. Dad dresses and makes us dress appropriately for each job we have to accomplish. He always said, "If you wear the right clothes, a worker can protect his body from the elements," by having Mom knit and buy plenty of boots, gloves, overalls, sleeves, shin guards, raincoats, and hats to match. My father's farm is one of the best-equipped farms in the South.

The days we work are scheduled accordingly. Monday is our starting day for the farm, Dad wears his overalls all day and sends us to school, if he had to come to our school house on a Monday, boy, he looked like an overworked horse on its last leg! Most Mondays consisted of looking after the West Side orchard, making sure the trees had enough fertilizer and that insects were not eating away at the trees. Mondays involved a complete spraying of the orchard and removal of caterpillars, grubs, and flies, the procedure is tiring. It makes the daylong running up and down ladders all day checking the fruit. It is a giving process, every time we find a new type of insect, Dad has Mom look it up in the farmer's encyclopedia to find out what kind of Insect it is and if it is dangerous to the crop or not. After Mom looks up the insect, Dad has to find a way to remove the insect from the crop.

Mr. Riley knows everything about the characteristics of insects and what to look for. He generally associates them to the type of crop they eat. Most of my father's knowledge of crops came from Grandpa's old journal books, Grandpa explained what happened to his crops on the field by making symbols. One symbol you did not like to see in Grandpa's journal book was a big X this means that whatever problem he had was so bad that it made his crops unsalvageable for the year. A large line with a R over it meant Grandpa had to replant. The two bad symbols seem to go hand and hand; if you saw one, you would surely see the other. Granddad mostly planted corn, wheat, and barely for miles square. If Dad found any bugs other than the ones that Granddad had marked in his ledger, an update was needed to the farm ledger, identifying what is wrong with the crops.

Tuesday is a walk through day. Dad, Mom, and Chip look over papers and sales receipts. Dad wears his house clothes all Tuesday long, an old pair of paints and gray shirt because his favorite clothes are all worn out by the sun. On Wednesday, it is livestock day. Dad walks around in his Texas getup, an old cowboy hat and leather front protectors. On Thursday, it is finishing the crops day and we are all back in our overalls and long johns. On Friday, it is take it easy day. They just called it that, because farmers never really have an easy day. Mom leaves a list of repairs on the kitchen table Dad, Chaney, and Chip set out to fix on the house. Every Friday afternoon, they put up gates, maintenance the barns, and chop the edging growth back around the farm.

Saturday, we all go to town to take orders from the flea market, Dad likes working his knickknack stand, he builds little knickknacks that look like statues twiddled from wood, he does this in his quite time. All of the work always gets done one way or another, in-between Mom looking for Dad all day and Dad looking for Mom all day. After waking up at daybreak, we come in from the field at night exhausted. No time is wasted on our Knox farm. Running the farm is not an easy task at all. All of the fruit has to be cleaned and the crops have to be well processed. Chip says, "No one going to pay for bad apples, so we being the family and hired workers have to look through all of the goods and verify, if it is ripe or not." that's That is how Chip would explain to the hands what to do. Chip likes to test his speeches on Chaney, Susan, and I to make sure that what he says is correct. It is funny to see Chip giving an enthusiastic speech about farming then just pointing and telling the hands to get it done.

Dad has a more direct approach to getting what he wants done. If they complain, he already has it written on his schedule so, in turn, Dad never has to tell anyone what needs to be done. It is already on the schedule, all they have to do is read it. One year, Dad throughout the whole crop of apples to the pigs, that is what we call it when you can only use your crop, as animal food because too many bugs have gotten into our crop. After eating apples for a month or two, the farm animals never looked so healthy and fat. If the crop really looks bad, then we use it as fertilizer. We lay down old shell rock that is dug up out of the query; it is crushed until it became a fine powder. This gets rid of the bugs. They turn into little white statues because the lie dries them up. Using too much of it makes the crop taste nasty and dry. The other alternative was to put pine in the soil before planting season. This worked well but it is expensive for us to get pine trees cut into cinders at the mill then the hands use two mules to cart the cinders from the mill to our Sycamore Place Knox Farm that is a good ways away.

Other means we use to culture the land involve chopped coal, ash, and wood. Using these remedies gets rid of unwanted bugs, to say the least it leaves debris on the planting field ground after harvesting season. We built scarecrows for each field to keep the birds and unwanted animals away. This is Chip's and

Susan's specialty, they like to put together a couple of boards and set up a scary face, especially in October. We also make fences to keep wolves and foxes out, Dad complained when the dirt got the best of the white wooden fences. Mom smoothed him over, so we would not have to clean and repaint the wooden fences every week. The fences consisted of twisted metal along the fence posts and picket fencing around the house to keep both dogs in Blue our basking hound, and Palm Palm our sheep dog. Blue and Palm Palm get out any of the way and run through the fields until eating time this was the time that everyone gathered at the house.

~Chapter 3~
Moving the Out House

Moving the Out House

Now Mom came into the house with a big grin that only spoke of problems for Dad and my brother Chipper. She said with sweat on the face, sweepingly out of breath "the outhouse for the women sure stinks." I just walked by and it really stank, most of the men go out to the back woods and get clean. The stench attracted bugs during the summer time so Dad and Chipper set out, walking towards the stench area, to move the outhouse across our field to another location. The Littles down the street have their outhouse on the top floor of their farmhouse with a neat contraption that allowed the waste to flow out through a wood shaft and into a metal barrel, which they later dumped out on the edge of the property. My Father said they had unnecessary work dumping the barrel and all; he did not want to say anything but, it put the crap smell in the air inside their house. This unwanted smell causes farmers to get sick because of the green type of mold that came along with it. Some mold is good and other molds are bad. That green type of mold is not the type of stuff we make cheese out of.

Every time that we moved the outhouse Dad and Chip set out on a mission to find the perfect place to dig a 7 to 9 foot hole and fill it 2 feet with crushed stone and flowers from the garden. We have to fill the soap pail and the water bucket every day for Mom and Susan. Dad gets a patch of the sweet smelling special stuff to sit in his wooden rocking chair out on the porch and smoke. He stands out by the outhouses and smokes away the awful smell. This time Dad called to Chipper and had him get a bucket, Dad said,

"This moving the outhouse is getting on my last nerve." Then he put the largest pail that he could find under a wooden seat that he made an oval cutout in to. Now, all we have to do is throw some wood thatch on top of the bucket and light it on fire. This seemed like a good idea at first.

We did the same with the men's outhouse and put it on the daily schedule to burn. The first month or so everything went well; we proceeded out with the burn cloth over our face dressed completely with the gloves, sleeves, and mask then took the buckets and burned the feces. After that month, no one wanted to burn the junk in the bucket, so they started dumping it out by the tree line and washing the bucket. Before long, the tree line started to smell. It was not even a good while before Dad caught hold of what was going on, the fact that we started to do things the lazy way may have gotten us in trouble. One day about two months later, Dad was walking by the tree line and smelled the mess. It made the air smell like an animal had died in the woods next to the rear house. When Dad smelled the bad smell, he held a family meeting that night. Dad said, "Who has been dumping the outhouse bucket at the tree line!" Dad was angry but not trying to show it. Every one put their heads down except Chaney.

Mom said, "It is all right as long as it is not near our house."

Dad did not like it at all. He started getting red in the face because he had made a special procedure for everything and if his procedure was not followed, we had a problem. No one was able to work on nothing else until Dad solved this problem.

"No, it is not all right!,"

Dad said. He usually does not go against Mom's wishes, but enough was enough for Dad. Now if we had an inside bathroom like the Little's, this would be no problem. Dad absolutely hated the idea of anyone taking a sit down in the house. He called it disgusting. It was unsanitary to him. His whole idea was to keep the sick away.

If you had put all of the cow manure in the haft at the end of the farm rows and then spread it out each day, in Dad's mind, cow manure was cleaner than the humans were. After Dad spoke his mind, everyone got silent and Dad's raised voice went down. He explained,

"I expect the best work out of all of you, even if it seems below your standards, to do a good job is what this farm needs". "People that are willing to do the most menial jobs, when I assign a task to get done, I expect it done, not for my telling you to do the job that way, but for the safety of all of you, children."

Poly ran into the serious conversation with her Miss Nancy doll and then ran out because Dad handed her the stare down. He was giving us the working hand you-did-something-wrong speech, then Chip broke a smile. Dad could not be angry no more, even though the wind was blowing the bad smell towards the house. Dad patted Chip on the butt and said, "Come on, Chip, we got some crap to cover up!" Chips little smile went away in a flash and they left. Then it was Moms turn to talk to Chaney, Susan and me. Mom said, "Please do not let your father down". "We expect better of you and if he tells you to do something, just do it his way, no questions asked". "He is a hardworking man trying to make it easy on you, children. You at least owe him your respect".

Chaney said, "I am glad he did not ask me go out there, that stuff surely stinks!"

Mom let out a laugh with her serious face falling short of a smirk. Then we all left out to help Dad and Chip, one for all and all for one. When Dad saw Chaney, Susan, and I come out, he handed off the pitchforks and shovels and shook his head as if to say this is just a two-person job. Chip had the wheelbarrow full of the good planting soil; my guess is by now Dad did not even care what they did to cover that God-awful smell up, as long as it went away.

We had seen the inner city children play a game with the teacher paddler. Every weekend, they are out playing at the local Market Place Field. When we go to town we saw the older children play a game in the field that involves hitting a spool of yarn covered in leather with a teacher paddler. After they hit the spool into the air, the hitter then runs around kitchen pads until they get back to the starting pad. At first, it was just one pad then they made it into four pads and called the one that the paddled stands at home base. We called it bat ball, Dad and Mom liked to call it rounders. The immigrants were playing this new New York game in the fields.

My brother, Chaney, got an idea just to go ahead and make our own game of it. He tore a pocket out of the old clothes in the barn and wrapped it around a ball of rope, found Mom's old baking paddle to use to hit the ball. Then he got Susan to lace the leather pocket with a little leather twine and it looked just like the one the big kids had.

Playing ball was fun because everyone had a job and their job was evident. Chaney's friends came over to play. They are fast. Evan had to be the fastest of all of Chaney's friends. He walked with a cane like an old man with a limp, but the day he came over to play ball, which he called baseball, he outran all the bases and Chaney's other friends, Sam Cook and Marlin Hays, half stood and watched limping Evan take every base. Chip would not play. He said, "I'm not getting hurt over that fool stuff." I was happy to be playing a game rather than doing work. We all stood out in the sun waiting for the ball to hit the ground. When it did, the batter ran around the bases as we tried to throw him out. When the ball came close, we tried to get it to first base as soon as possible.

The lead runner ran out to get to home base before the ball got to him. If the person who gloved the ball did not throw the ball hard enough to reach first base before the lead runner reached first base, they had to let the runner stay on the base. If the batter could round all three bases before we could throw the ball to the person at the base, then the runner could score home. This is what Evan did. If the person with the ball got to him before the runner got to home plate, they would be called out. This game was catching on in the South. We were just getting related to it, while the inner city kids were playing the game better and better every time we would see them.

We played rounders with our friends from around the neighborhood. I have traveled up to three miles to get to the next farm to play this game. It is a fun game to play, but it is hard to organize; sometimes we just throw the ball around. Walking back and forth to see our friends sometimes, we meet in the middle or at the schoolhouse. It is always a trip to meet up with all of our friends. We never did too much hanging at the schoolhouse because Miss Parity may be there and ask us to complete some chores. After doing the farm work and homework from school, it feels good to be a child again and play.

~Chapter 4~
The Broken Buggy Wheel

The Broken Buggy Wheel

My family has a horse buggy to repair. While Dad and Mr. Riley where out working on the farm Dad wanted to clear some space for the wheat to sit before processing. Dad had to sift the wheat to clean it and process the seeds. When he and Mr. Riley had pulled the buggy out of the barn to make space, there was a large rock that our horses, Sundance and May, skimmed past and the buggy wheel hit the side of the rock. That horse buggy ran upside of a rock and the left front wheel cracked. My father and Mr. Riley ran inside, got a steel plate from the grinder box in the tool shed, and went to work.

They first bent the metal plate to the curve of the buggy's wheel. Then they fastened wood scrap to make a smoother ride. The wheels we had on the buggy were made of solid wood with a fork in the middle. Well, Dad and Mr. Riley fastened the wood together and then harnessed the four horses to the buggy May, Sundance, Willie and Marcy. After readying the buggy, Mr. Riley and Dad rode the buggy around the farm path that went in a huge circle. The fixing they did made the whole buggy limp and wobble back and forth. It looked like a duck in the heat of July.

Smith and Duncan made the buggy, so Dad had to get in touch with Smith to fix the awkward wheel problem. Smith and Duncan is a horse sales and specialty wagon builder located in Nashville, Tennessee. They gave us a good price on the wagon, it cost two of the large president bill notes that Mom keeps in her purse. This is what it costs to get the wagon fixed. The last time it broke, was some years back. Dad had Chip and Chaney pack the grocery cart to prepare for the trip to Nashville. Dad was ready to leave immediately before anything else went wrong with the buggy.

Mr. Riley was standing in front of the house when Dad told him to take care of things while he was gone. Dad said, "Tell the hands to continue on what they left off yesterday." Mr. Riley waved us off and Dad left the dogs in the yard. Usually, Mr. Riley would come by and take care of their food every day we were away, and we left to Nashville.

Chip conducted the grocery cart that Susan, Chaney, and I rode in. Dad was steering the carriage with Mom and Poly and up the winy road to Nashville, we went. Along the way, it got dark and Dad pushed on, hoping no one would bother us on the way. We passed by several different strange characters. Chaney kept Chip's rifle close by, covering both the buggy and the grocery cart at the same time. We looked like a poor family moving because of the Civil War. Riding the dark road was bumpy because Chip could not see the dips and rocks; not even with a lantern. It was hard to see the signs that pointed toward Nashville, especially with the broken buggy in front of us. Poly and I were dropped off at Uncle Nick's place. Mom, Chip, Susan, and Chaney went in to town with Dad to stay a night in the Grand hotel.

The next day, Dad let Chip, Susan, and Chaney walk the town while he and Mom took the broken buggy into the repair shop of Smith and Duncan. See, Mr. Smith was a well-aged wrinkled face man with a big grin. He had a dark complexion from staying in the sun too long. Mr. Duncan was a fancy guy, who liked to put little art work on the buggies to make them look more exclusive. Everything Mr. Duncan worked on had to be elegant. He is one of those Northerners that learned three or four good words and stuck with them.

After they all came back to Uncle Nick's place, Dad went to put the buggy into the storage shack by the barn at Uncle Nick's house. Chipper, Chaney, and Susan went back to Nashville City while I (Chris) and Poly stayed at Uncle Nick's and Aunt Sara's house. They lived in a country house right outside of town. Uncle Nick is a skilled cobbler, he is good at his trade. Those types of trades' man usually lived up North and sell their products to big stores, but Uncle Nick liked to keep it to a small shop in the inner city called Nick's Shoes on Main Street in Nashville. The minute we got to Uncle Nick's house, Mom and Dad told us to stay out of trouble. My cousin, Lou Ann, and her younger brother, William, liked to run around outside the house. This made four of us children running around outside making noise. First, we played tag and then we played catch with a ball; after that, we climbed the trees and hung upside down. William is just about my age. He is funny, always making fun of something. At his age, most children do not notice all of those he notices. William steadily makes fun of the new bike with the three wheels. "If man was meant to ride on three wheels, he would not have to run on a pedal for it." Another time, William said his "dog, Poncho, could eat like a horse." Then he feed Poncho some water and barley; the dog did look like a horse at a horse trough. I am glad Poncho could chew the barley up. I know my teeth cannot even begin to get through that tough stuff.

We only stayed at Uncle Nick's house for a day or two but it seemed like an hour; before long, Dad had Chip and Chaney packing the buggy and grocery cart to head home. The next morning, we left to head home. The wheel was fixed and the buggy ran smoothly. Poly, Mom, and I rode inside the carriage, while Susan rode upfront with Dad. Chip and Chaney drove ahead of us in the grocery cart. Dad got all six horses going again and we only had to make one stop to feed the horses. Chip and Chaney ran around with the boot, giving them some water and a little hay. There is no one on the trail today, just a man selling fruit and the manor house that we pasted on the smooth easy ride home. Riding in the buggy is better than riding in the grocery cart because I get to look out the windows and make faces in the rear mirror between the two oval rear-looking glasses. Mom likes to keep her head down; she may have had a bad experience or two riding in the carriage. Mom did not like to talk to us about her past life; she is a woman of today.

~Chapter 5~
About Chaney

About Chaney

Chaney is only fourteen and he has a knack for counting. I guess it all started when he and Chipper would bet on things around the farm. Chipper, who always worked close with Dad, is going on sixteen. The girls always came by and tried for him. As soon as they get marriage age, Mom said, "A strapping young fellow like Chipper could sweep the princess away and never be seen again." Chaney looked like one of those inner city ruffians, you know the type that could rob a bank and then sit on the corner eating ice cream because he was so cool, as cool as they come. Chaney is always up for a good bet. Dad used to joke with his friends and say,

"Watch out for Chaney, you might lose your shoes hanging around with him"; "Do not drop anything in front of Chaney, it will never come back."

My guess is that he was going to become a con man or casino jockey. Our uncles come looking for Chaney, he shows them a new card trick or how to cheat. Chaney likes to ride the horses around the farm circle. He could make Sun Dance look like a trick horse. Dad never liked spoiling the horses but Chaney would pick one, teach it to rope, and do his fancy prance. Chaney only feed them carrots for their tricks; he is not mean to the horses. He and Susan hang out in the grassing area riding horses over staples. This is special to Susan. They both dress in their parlor clothes and run the horses until they noticed who they are.

No one wanted to be a farmer in Tennessee. The work was hard and the life was harder. Chaney wanted a way out; he just had not found the direction yet. Most of his friends were the gigolo type. This was awkward for Dad because Chaney had too many women on his plate. Every week he found a new one. Too many older women wanted to get acquainted with Chaney; he had the look the older women wanted to subdue. They liked the tough guys in the South and being wartime, women looked for protection rather than the nice face to come home to. This made all the difference to the women in the South a tough man meant that they could still go on with their life when the fight came their way it was pick a side and report. Otherwise the war has just started it was General Robert Lee who hand chose who he wanted to travel North.

Chaney wanted to leave immediately and fight for his side but dad told him that this was just going to be a scrimmage right afterwards everything would go back to normal. There were the jumpers that only fought to be in a fight and those who wanted slavery to end. Others just fought to make the pay. I hear dad talking about the war and telling us about the black man in the North that lived in the white neighborhood that started it. He was supposed to be returned and was not returned because the North said he was part of their community. Afterwards the fighting started up when an owner went to get back civil servant there was a fight and they started coming home from the North empty handed, if they came back at all. People started to protest and rethink their ways because the United States Government outlawed slavery and the

South kept their slaves. Who was supposed to account for the scrimmages, the South made an army that was headed by Robert Lee to get the slaves back.

I am confused about the president but he had problems with Tennessee because our politician Andrew Johnson was well known in these parts so in respect for him most of the Tennessee North released theirs. This started people staying to their selves in tight communities for protection. My father talked a whole bunch about the fights with his friends everyone was uptight and tried to ignore the whole problem. Listening to dad get excited about the whole thing made us children not want to think about the issue. Chaney being an expert gun man wanted to show off his skills and leave the South because he acted like a Northerner following in grand pa's footsteps, farm work was not in his favor and it was not his favorite thing to do. Chaney liked women and liked showing off. He wanted to fight for whoever accepted him his friends went with the South and have yet to come home. Dad ended up changing both Chips and Chaney age on the census so they would not qualify for civil duty to make sure nether deserted him. I know that the North send messages to the town requesting a person or two but no one went because they said this was for the north to protect against the people who kept slaves illegally.

~Chapter 6~
Civil War

Civil War

Uncle Owen Henry left from Pennsylvania to help fight in the war against civil servant use. My dad always blamed the big plantation owners for the cost of food being too high, too many towns started to farm their own crops. In the South, we had plantations that went for thirty miles at a time. The Union Soldiers kept burning them down, from Northern Virginia and the South wanted it stopped. General Jackson wrote a newsletter to the South explaining how, by burning the plantations, he was cleansing the South and building an *equal* United States. Living in the Confederate South meant many people, especially the old plantation owners, did not like the Northerners burning their fields and crops. This was what General Lee called pillaging our members.

The food shortage was evident. My father had a privately owned farm. His workers got paid a wage and many more people came to work, black and white alike they all wanted to make wages to pay for land, food, and clothing for their children. Sharecroppers traveled to Tennessee from all over, looking to start a new life with all of their belongings on their back. Many were ransacked by Indians and had nothing to their name. The people that were thrown off of their land for owning plantations were older and had no place to live. Most of the blacks said that President Lincoln was making life harder for them because many crow laws were made to protect blacks, the plantation owners had started to rent land out to them for outrageous prices, making it hard for blacks to survive in the South. Others opened their own towns and lived with one another.

Uncle Owen sends us postcards that Dad travels to town to pick up, telling us about how they liberate slaves by the thousands. Dad likes to read Uncle Owen's postcards to us aloud. Every time Dad gets a postcard from Uncle Owen, he has what we call a family sit-down the same night he receives the postcard. Dad said,

"Our Uncle Owen is a great man who fights for good reasons."

Having two presidents made it hard to understand what was going on but President Davis of the confederate South was a well-educated man. He wrote elegantly and had purpose to his words, when it came to the bottom line, Dad said that we can *no longer own people* it is just not right. To have an unpaid servant is just not right; *people are meant to live by their hard work and sweat, not by their color.* I thought this was true because when slaves got too old to work, the plantation owners did not know what to do with them. Many were sent away and traveled north while, others lived in shacks next to the fields that they worked on and sit every day to look over the property of the owner. For plantation owners, making a living with no expenses was coming to an indefinite end. This put pressure on the local farmers to produce more crops with larger fields; having larger fields meant having to hire more help. Dad tried to stay away from what he called commodity crops because the people depended on them and these types of crops overused the land. Peanut, cotton, and potato are the largest fields in the South. You could not plant nothing else on the land for the incoming season. These type of farmers own more land to keep their crops growing by rotating fields. We had an increased number of jobless carpetbaggers. They came pouring into Tennessee like a rain that would not stop. Too many in the South did not want to buy anything from the plantations. My family said that the big plantations are what makes average, every day workers poor.

They owned the food stores so they charged whatever suited their pockets and what suited their pockets did not suit ours.

The plantations started to sell land and my father bought a little land here and a little land there. He put up signs that said "Equal pay for equal work" and the North's armies left his property alone. It all started when I was four. I would get to running around and, all of a sudden, the breath would come out of my mouth, stand next to me and never come back. Every time it happened, a different adult had a prescription for it. Dad said,

"Boy you caught the virus!"

and then Chip came up with

"The wind was knocked out of you" theory.

Mom had a big bottle of syrup waiting for me inside she gave me a spoonful and sent me to bed for a while. Dad said,

"Hand the boy the syrup."

It was mixed with a little of Dad's corn liquor. When Poly started up with the same problem, they had to treat her with the same serum. That made me feel better because I was not the only stupid that is what Chaney called it. Chaney said, "That stuff is for old people on their last leg. Young yens do not have those types of problems. We spit tobacco around the farm and kick the dirt, but nothing makes me sick. Dad ordered the doctor to come out. He pulled up in his fancy carriage with presidential throws on it; red, white, and blue banners that lit the carriage up, along with a balding man named Mr. Andy White and his wife, Victoria. They knocked on the door. Dad and Mom lead them in the house. The doctor had his black doctoring bag while his wife had a stethoscope around her neck and a wooden tomahawk. They both came inside, looked around for a minute, and sat in the living room.

"How is everything, Mr. Henry?" Mr. White said.

Dad responded, "Can't be no better. Cows out producing milk, crops look good this year, and my second to oldest son, Chaney, is about to graduate scholars".

"Susan has come to be helpful around here Poly and Chris are always doing their, How about yourself, Doc?"

Dr. White responded, "No complaints.

This smallpox virus has been going around; have to keep them teens under twenty-four-hour watch at the hospital. Where is everybody?" asked Doctor White as he looked around to see the whole family.

Dr. White was right to ask this question because there was always someone at home. Dad answered, "Well, Poly and Susan are upstairs and the boys went over to the house of their friend, Mr. Cook's son, Samuel, to play rugby."

Mrs. Victoria went to the kitchen with Mom. They both liked to swap recipes every time they saw each other. Mom had a big pitcher of lemonade waiting for Dr. White. Mom, walking toward the kitchen, said, "Did you see the recipe in the newspaper last week, Vicky?" Mom went on, "It came out a little runny; Then, we drained the pasta off and mixed it in the cheese."

"I had to throw it out. It was too runny," Mrs. Victoria answered Mom.

They sounded like best friends who have been away from each other for a long time. Mom made a fuss over Doctor White. Patricia was her best friend, but Victoria was quickly moving in on Patricia's friendship spot. Dr. White drove his carriage from Knox County Hospital to see me. That was a little over a mile. Chaney, with his sick boy routine, was getting old.

"Doctor! Doctor! I can't breathe! I've got this dirt patch stuck in my throat and can't get it out! I really could not help it. The air would get tight and then I would become lite headed. I have to take little breaths when I needed to take big ones. I ran in and Mom overhugged me, making me look like a woozy. I thought it was better to take the old man's medicine and Dad agreed. Then Dad and Dr. White stopped talking and the latter said,

"Where is your son, let us take a look at him."

Dad responded, "He is on the steps over there. Come here, Chris!"

I walked over because Mom disallowed running in the house. "So you say every once in a while you lose your breath? Now, open your mouth for me, Chris." Then, Dr. White stuck a stick in my mouth.

"Say ah", I repeated,
"Ah ahh."

Afterwards, he turned to my father and said, "This must be a seasonal thing. Has it been happening often on and off or all year around?" I told him it happens when the air gets dry around springtime.

He responded, "Yes." Then he turned to my father and said,

"It must be an acute asthmatic condition. Make sure he drinks plenty of water during the dry months."

Dad called into the kitchen to Mom and told her to get his whisky canteen from the china closet. Mom and Victoria stood next to the kitchen door with the canteen in her hand. I walked up and thanked Mom. I then started outside to fill it up. As soon as the canteen left Mom's hand, Dad yelled,

"Do not let this canteen out of your sight! Keep it with you everywhere!"

It would be hard to lose; the canteen had Dad's name inscribed on both sides, "Property of Mr. Henry Smith." It looked like a tin. I went outside, dumped it in the bucket of water, and took a swig. Now, this looked fancy; how many nine-year-olds get to drink from a real liquor bottle?

After being outside and watching the sun go down, I came back inside to see Doctor White and his wife sitting on our bench in the study. Dad was holding Poly with Susan on the curved part of the bench talking to Mrs. Victoria. Mom came in from the kitchen with fresh cookies on a plate and lemonade in the pitcher. As soon as she asked, Dr. White said, "Why, thank you."

Dad slipped him some money for looking at Poly and me. Then they saw Poly looking confused and laughed. "Is not she just the most adorable thing!" Mrs. Victoria said.

Mom answered, "Yes, and only three!" While putting the pitcher down on the reading table, she shoved a plate of cookies in every one's laces. Mom was the perfect hostess. Before long, Chip and Chaney came in playing with a medicine ball.

"Not in the house, boys," Dad said.

Chip shook Doctor White's hand while Chaney waved and said hello. They both went back out the front door with the black ball. Dr. White said, "We better be going before nightfall." He and his wife walked out and hopped on the front of his horse carriage. With one "Yeah," them heading away into the sunset.

I like to play in the forest and see the wind moving the trees and the tree limbs swaying with the whistle of fresh air, flowing through the grass and trees. I would be running as if the trees were trying to catch me. While I ran, the trees reached out as I moved as fast as the wind blows. The deer next to the house forage along, almost looking like men lined up for a search party. The white-tailed deer came around. They liked to pick fruit off Mom's garden trees. They had a time getting to the actual orchard because my Mom kept wire fencing around it. Down the hill was a hut Poly and I like to play. It was made of sandstones that are mortared together with clay, an original baker house. Dad and Mom like to use the woodstove in the kitchen.

The workers used the hut to weld in and do blacksmith work. I'd go running and Poly would go running after me, moving her three-year-old feet as fast as she could. After school, I'd go down to the creek to gather washing water in a pail. I only carried one pail at a time. Chip and Chaney carried four on a mop stick. Everything they did they had to do better than me. Running around in the forest while gathering prickles all over my play clothes are some of the fun things we did. Too many deer foraged in the woods. This made me smell musky just like a deer by the time I went home. I would see raccoon, possum, rabbit, snake, and even skunk down by the creek while fetching water. Dad used the well in the front of the house; he would only fish the creek during the month catfish are abundant.

Over the summer months, Dad would go to the hatchery to gather fish eggs to throw into our little pond on the other side of the farmland. Geese and ducks like to play in the water. This made it a good place to push the little boat out and sleep on it. After church on Sundays, you could see my father sleeping on the boat. He would sit on the boat with his hat down and let the water pull him back and forth, as the geese made noise at the lake. Mom cooked chicken more than the goose. When we have a goose, it was all we had to eat the whole day. We ate small portions of food in the house on Sundays, waiting for the big feast. The woods get dark at night so dark you could not see your hand in front of your face.

As the wind comes from the northeast in October, the cool, chilled air of the start of winter becomes evident. The tip of your nose turns red as the wind gust multiplies to push you around from each and every direction. The bending trees sway back and forth making noises. First, you hear the leaves rustle, then you hear a tree bark make a sound, something like a screech one hears from a castle door being opened. Downed trees point us to paths in the backwoods that lead to headings on the farm. During October, the oak and sycamore leaves turn red, yellow, orange, green, brown, and purple, giving meaning to fall as if Mother Nature is sending a warning to us that the weather is changing, to say hello to Jack Frost, who has traveled far but is on his way. The summer months are hot and sticky during the day, and cool and breezy at night. Thunderstorms come in abundance during spring. Lightning strikes hit the ground with large crackling sounds, as if men in the clouds were ripping fine print paper. Lightning streaking through the sky, making its mark as it webs over the earth, only wanting to come down when it has found the perfect spot to do so, shoves the middle of the trees, pushing them in until they fall down. The Lightning always taking away the highest point, as if to say,

"You are not going to stand taller than I do",

The wind, rain, and lightning teaming up the trees to bully them into surrender, forcing one to hide for cover.

~Chapter 7~
Elements

Elements

Rain brings new beginnings, new times that renew the earth rainbows that renew the land. I always thought if Isaac Newton were sitting under the apple tree when the apple fell on his head, it must have been because of a rainstorm. Every spring, lightning and thunder, make such sound until the ground gets too thick to walk on and the air smells like grass. The creek overflows, the trees push back on our water channels until they are blocked with debris from the trees and leaves.

Well, back to Newton, he must have been in a rainstorm that he had to cover his head with the tree and then the apple fell on his head. Gravity, he said, taking a bite out of the apple he must have thought,
"I need to net the tree off for worms",
while picking his teeth and thinking about how to explain this new force that pushes down and makes us short. We weave the net and even it out with a pitchfork, spooler, and a knitting pin, and then the bugs go away. Well, I have seen mud and mud has seen me; we get our boots on and go out in it to galosh around, then we run and slid in it. All just fun, Mom complains every time.

You had better get your overalls on and your work clothes ready to be cleaned by supper or the mud will stiffen up the long johns and overalls and everywhere you go, puffs of dust from the dry mud will appear. It helps to pat on your overalls until they make smoke signals better than the Indians.

If we had a way about it, I would say that the fall storms were worse than the spring. Dad put up a whistle tube and this device would tell us if the wind was dangerous for the farm animals or not. Mom told him,

"Let them go,"

but Dad, Chaney, and Chip would go outside and rustle up some steer then put them in the barns to keep them safe. My guess is that mud seems to go with rain. When the rain falls all so gentle, it barely touches the dirt and little droplets of indentured earth are seen as darkened imprint on the ground just before the big rain comes. It always leaves just enough time to run inside. After getting inside near shelter before the rain gears up, it pours down in waves of larger droplets that resemble the way honey runs off a sickle, specked in intervals of three-second crisps droplets of rain that smack you wet when they land on your face. This type of rain forces you to pull down your cover and let the water fall off, making a sheet in front of your eyes. Rain must have bought off mud because every time it rains, the mud gets thick. Mud so thick that it makes you slip until it gathers in front of your boots to suddenly stop you from sliding. Just when you lean back ready for a fall, suddenly, you are standing straight up. The mud that, when running, you fall and slide on, with your feet out and hands down, waiting to stop only to laugh at yourself, while everyone else is laughing at you, too. The type of mud that makes the dogs growl and the horses pant, when you try to take them out in it.

Yes, mud is a funny thing. It comes in different colors, textures, and moistures. The dark stuff seems to be too thick to walk on even when you have boots strapped to your feet. As you walk the shoe print disappears not able to see the water slurping into the shoe print until it covers your foot. Then it sucks your foot in, almost pulling off your boot after it grabs the boot. You then see the water rush in over the top part of your shoe, making a slurping noise, then a pop when you finally get your foot out of the darkened mud. The red stuff is impossible to get out of, the clay substance that holds the earth together does not like to negotiate with boots that smash it down. This type of mud is just not made for children to run on. At the top of it, it is smooth like sliding on ice; once you put weight on it, you can kiss your boots good-bye. The brown stuff that you make mud pies out of and fling at each other is the only type of mud I like to deal with: It is predictable in every way. We even run and slide on it and it dries off your clothes in flakes, but once shaken off, your clothes look new.

I came into the schoolhouse at 7:30 A.M. to make 8:00 A.M. class. My sister, Susan, and brother, Chaney, were talking with Mary, Jesse, Theresa, and James, the teen age group, so I galloped ahead of them, heading toward the elm tree in front of the schoolhouse. I took off running. My friends, Peter and Sandra, must have been late, or I was early. When I got to the school, Miss Parity handed me a broom. This was usually the girl's job, but I dare not complain. Next, I went into making a dust frenzy, until Miss Parity told Rhonda to show me how to sweep.

"Rhonda, please show little Christopher how to sweep."

"Yes, Ma'am,"

Rhonda said and the next thing I knew, she was doing the sweeping for me.

"Okay, Chris, this is how you sweep a floor," Rhonda said. "First, you press on the thatch part of the broom; then after the wheat part bends, you push the broom until the wheat bristles stand straight up.
Now, you try it."

At this time, my brother Chaney and sister Susan came in the schoolhouse door.
"What are you doing, Chris, trying to make friends with Rhonda?" Chaney said making a kissing face, with a grin. "She is too old for you.", Chaney all the sudden looked concerned.
"Hi, Chaney!" Rhonda said. She was twelve years old—two years younger than Chaney was.
Chaney said to her,
"Hey, why you got my little brother doing the sweeping? He needs to go outside and fetch sticks like usual. That sweeping not for him."
It seemed Chaney could get away with anything. There were only four brooms in the schoolhouse, with about thirty gals there for school. They wouldn't miss me one bit. Most of the boys' fathers complained that their sons did not need schooling to take over their farmland. My Dad said,
"Get your smarts because you are going to need them."
Every week, he sent Chaney to school with nine dollars for the teacher. I guess that was the going rate for school a dollar a day for each child.
I always thought it was book money because we always got the best books to read. Sometimes I grabbed Shakespeare. Other times, I got to read

Moby Dick and another time I read a book I did not even understand, like *New System of Chemical Philosophy* a rugged old book that was passed around in the class, to make the older children look smart. With thick browned pages one would think a wizard was reading it when he created a black cloud then snuck out the door without a clue. Out of all the books in the class, the one I liked the most was *Moby Dick*. Every week, we had to switch books, so I would copy the last passage I read on to a ledger sheet to remember where I had left off. Dad always looked concerned because it seemed that I had more homework than my brother or sister Susan. I read efficient enough for a nine year old. Shuddering slowly through some chapters that had big words that I did not understand then read fast in other areas of the book, Mom would make me reread until it sounded smooth. I like to blame not being able to work around the farm on my having too much schoolwork. This was okay by Dad as long as he saw good grades in the teacher's grade book. The minute he saw a bad letter, it was back to farm work for me. Get this and fill that Dad would show me not to play around during school. Schooling was important to Dad and he had a no-play-around attitude about it. Susan would help me until Mom got the stop-cheating-look on her face. She would pick up the dusting brush, slap it on the table, then say,

"Christopher, do your own learning!"
My name always became long when I was in trouble.

Grandfather did not look old for his age. He was sixty-four but looked twenty-eight. Granddad is a fun person to be around. Dad said the old man was hard and bitter when he was growing up. Granddad seemed too nice to be the way Dad explained him. As hard as my father looked, everyone expected to see an old-looking squint-eyed man with a gunner's overcoat and spiffy custard boots, but what they got was a little short man with a top hat and sales pitch. His wife must be ten years younger than my Mom. Grandma Mary looked a head older than Susan. When he would come down, he liked to stay in Nashville, next to Uncle Nick. Him and Dad never did see eye to eye. This was a North executive who worked for R.H. Macy merchandise incorporation, buying all up and down the east coast. If he found a good product, he would buy it out for R.H. Macy and merchandise it for as long as he could. Every time he came around. Grandfather always promised to send something back from the North. I would not hold my breath because it would never come. The thought of getting big city products made me excited just listening to Grandpa's stories was enough for me. He talked about wars and people getting in trouble with the law. His stories were worth a million bucks. All of us children would sit for hours listening to Grandpa talk about his soldier days and him protecting his farm in Pennsylvania way before the Civil War was even thought of. Grandpa liked the fast life. After being on his farm for nearly thirty-seven years, he got himself a job with Rowland Hussey Macy. Mr. Macy was a friend of my grandfather. He called him Robert Smith. Mr. Macy gave my grandfather a job in contracting deals rather than the factory, to find tradesmen who could build, smith, do arts and crafts, and Grandpa would buy it at bulk price.

They used all types of cargo to move products around. Grandpa always talked about the new trains making it easier to travel and move products.

Grandpa already bought his stock in Vanderbilt New York Central Railways. Talking to Mr. Thomas from Pennsylvania, Grandpa also bought stock in the Pennsylvania, Baltimore/Ohio that they had just begun to look over the plans. Dad was not just going to buy into something that he could not use. Dad researched what was being built in the South and ended up not buying into railroads but grocery stores. This way, he always had a company to sell his farm goods, too.

Grandpa was a fast moving nothing last long, you had-better-enjoy-it type of person. The fact that a sales pitch and a nice face can take you a long way was true for Grandpa. He received his education late and latter went to PIT University to receive his bachelor's degree. Granddad never explained what subject he went to school for, but he had his degree. Dad is proud of him. These days, any schooling meant you were a manager and not just an average employee. Mom really did not like the fact that Granddad's wife

was so young. It bothered Mom because he always rubbed it in on my father that he could have a little brother thirty-five years younger than him. My father would get red and say, "My son could be that boy's daddy."

Grandpa has a little one in the oven about six months. Dad considers this irresponsible. Granddad may not last long enough to see the boy off to school, so Dad told Mom to put down another child on the census sheet just in case. Between Uncle Nick, Uncle Owen, and my father, Henry, they will find a way to take care of another one.

Father said there are only two types of people in this town: workers and procrastinators. The ones that work do too much work and the ones that do not work do too little of just about nothing. The do-nothings are the ones that sit back and pay everyone else to do their jobs. They have to have more land to make up for the difference from what they pay others. It has been about three years now; they all have either moved on and sold their land or let their unpaid workers go. Everyone here gets an average payday for an average day's work.

Sycamore Farm Knox, Tennessee, is the fairest place in the world. If you need work, there is plenty of opportunity for it here. We have schools and shops in town. There are farms all around us. Other places to work are the butcher shop, barbershop, liquor venue, cigar shop, the print shop, the Five and Dime, the hardware store, the Round Up club, the Knox Bank, and the Susie Inn. With the trains coming soon, they need local people to work on laying track. Another set of jobs are available at the lumberyard, steel mill, and being a train conductor. These new types of transportation produce a number of jobs. A third set of jobs consist of sheriff and deputy officer, local Knox Fire Department, and working for Knox Hospital. As you can see, there are many jobs in this southern town; they just need people working them.

Our population is thin, and our work force is thinner. This is a small town community of about 5000 whole. More and more people are moving north to stay out of the way of the Civil War. When you hear about the stories of crops being burned, such as Richmond and Manassas, Virginia. They say the fight is fierce. Most average men with families are trying to avoid the war by sending north. Others have gone out for the regiments but most people in Knox just plain let their unpaid workers go. The unpaid workers usually come back as sharecroppers, even though there is not a lot of money in renting farmland. When you think of all of the expenses associated with paying rent for land, it just makes it a hard life for blacks.

Father and his friends do not want trouble coming around town so they hire as many family men as possible. I have seen two or three blacks come through. Dad put them to work and I can tell you that their work is just as good as anybody else's is. The people around here are generous people; you just have to understand where they come from. They like to keep it clean, and most of our neighbors have family in the North; they just do not see traveling to get in a fight with their own kin. Some are adamant that President Davis has his way and go all out for the Civil War while others do not agree with President Davis him at all but are stuck where they are at because they do not own anything but this Southern land and, without that, they have nothing but their family. With Vice President Johnson living in East Tennessee and General Grant securing two forts in Tennessee, we have an impartial state that follows whomever they want to, one talks about the war in Tennessee except political figures.

~Chapter 8~
Going to the Market

Going to the Market

It is mid-July. You know, the hot month Father, Mom, Chaney, Susan, Poly, and I got ourselves ready to go to the market in Knoxville. Chip and Susan shared a horse. Chaney rode by himself. Dad, Mom, Poly, and I got into the cart and traveled by horse. The cart is full ready for sales the minute we left Willie and Marcy took to the road. When our whole family finally arrived, we all drank some water as Chip and Chaney tied down the horses and blocked the cart. A conspicuous crowd grew in the middle of Knoxville Main Street. There, in the middle of the roadway a young man struggled with a fairly large dark-haired shopkeeper with a white smock on. The young man had long blond hair, straggly–looking, with a dirty face. As far as I could see, the shopkeeper was holding on to the feisty, scrubby guy as if a fight had broken out and they were throwing the unwanted visitor out to the curb. A couple of townsmen jumped in to help after a little struggle. They finally pinned the straggly guy down. With dust rising off the road and a couple of horses starting to get restless, they had caused enough confusion for the day.

The people looked up in arms. Chaney ran over just about thirty feet away. I followed Chaney and Chip over, we made a hop and skip. Dad turned to see what Mom asked him about.

"Over here, honey!" and we were off to the races. After reaching the scene, "What is going on?" Chaney asked a wrinkled man in gray overalls.

The man, who was standing in a position not to let anything pass him by, answered back, "They caught a hooter stealing some goods from Mr. Thurman's gun batik."

Wow, the townspeople got hot real quick! This type of commotion did not usually happen in our little town square road. They had gotten hot! I noticed a petite woman with a pink bonnet on standing next to Chaney as if she was married to him. Chaney always liked to play dumb until you got to know him; then, you would find out that he is the smartest wiper snapper in the town. That is exactly what women do around wartime, throw themselves at eligible bachelors. Lonely women stand next to men to see how they look together. She waved her arm out with a handkerchief floating in the air to be escorted across the street. Being the gentleman that Chaney was, he disappeared off to coast the lovely lady across. Then he joined up and came back over to where Chip and I were standing with the perfume-covered handkerchief. Just a couple minutes later, Sherriff Grey arrived.

Breaking through the crowd, he grabbed the little guy and preceded to run the man in.

"Okay, now stand straight up all of y'all let the youngen go!"

Sherriff Gray said in his big man voice. His deputy came running up, grabbed one arm, then Sheriff Gray grabbed the other,

"To the jail you go now! You done picked the wrong shopkeeper to steal from today," Sheriff Gray said, while holding the young man into his body to

71

stop him from yanking back and forth to loosen their grip.

Sheriff Gray belted the boy one on his head. The townsfolk wanted to teach the young man a lesson but Sheriff Gray was impartial. He said, "We are going to try this man in front of a jury." They pulled on him tight and walked him to the jailhouse.

As we moved away, Chip said,

"The Knox people do not mob for any reason." Chaney responded, "If you steal, do not get caught because they are looking for a mater."
The Civil War was making everyone in Tennessee uncertain about the way they stand for rights and who they supported.
Mom, Dad, and Poly stayed next to the cart while I walked along with Chip and Chaney. I wanted to be just as big as them but my short skinny self only put smiles on the elder people's faces as they thought Chip was my father. We all walked further down the road and went into the local shop for candy. Chip bought an elmer pickle, Chaney and I bought two-nickel bags of Goodies hard candy. "That will be thirteen cents. Tell your mom and dad not to stay away now," Mr. Paterson, the shop owner, said as we left the store, nodding our heads "Yes, Sir." Leaving out,I noticed that everyone had already set up. You could not see the street anymore, it was covered with everybody's goods all around.

"Come on, let's hurry!"
Chaney said, and then all of us started to walk fast though the bazaar displays. By the time we got to our stand, the line for fresh fruit was long, so we slipped in back and started stocking more, moving fruit from the cart to the table.

Dad said,
   "You boys stay out of that trouble. Stay away, you hear!"

We all nodded and kept on working our little stand. Dad looked disappointed that we got involved in the town trouble. He knew that Chip and Chaney could hold their own. I think he did not like the fact that I was hanging with the big boys instead of heaving with Mom and by their wishes.
   Susan and Poly sat on the cart while Mom and Dad sold the fruit that we had brought to the market. They all had their straw weave bags ready for the fruit. Dad had the old white fruit scale out ready for the buyers. It looked like a seesaw with weights on one side and a pan on the other. Dad kept it out even though we did not use it. Around about noon, we closed down and cleaned up. Then we put a sign up that the stand would open again at one P.M. until three o'clock. It was about a twenty-minute ride home to restock. When we had gotten home, the dogs were outside, barking at a rabbit running around in the yard. Blue had his head down sniffing around, while our sheep dog, Palm Palm, barked loud.
   Dad yelled,
   "Be quit, dog!" as we passed by going at creep. Dad pulled the cart Chip, Chaney, and Susan came riding in on horses looking like bugle boys on the range. We ate sandwiches that Mom and Susan had made this morning and stored in the icebox.
   After eating a little lunch and waiting for Dad's prayer, we extended into a little work line, passing potato sacks of fruit to each other. The work line made the thirty-five-minute job into a fifteen-minute job. Then we hopped on the wagon and waited for

73

Mom and Poly. Poly needed her diaper cloth changed. Mom could not let her have a wet diaper, plus Susan was feeding Poly earlier.

Mom and Poly hopped on the wagon. I was already in the rear and Chaney had left for the market place a few minutes before us. Chip and Susan rode the same horseback they took off with Chip's big yaw leaving us in their dust. Dad let out a big laugh because those two liked to ride horses the same way as the professionals do.

Along the Apple Orchard Trail, we went to Knoxville the back way. This was a bumpy ride for the cart. We arrived in town at about 1:05 P.M. and started getting the fruit stand back up again. The lines formed and sales went as usual. The market had plenty of neat stuff: rocking chairs, table sets, glass goods, farm goods, and knitted items. The best thing there to me was the wooden toy stand. Mr. Baker kept all kinds of neat little wooden toys, such as wooden army men, dolls made by Mrs. Baker, the new trains, little play guitars, and whistles. After asking Mom for thirty cents for a whistle, Mom said, "Not this weekend." No bickering with Mom. What she says is as good as stone.

By the field area, the auction took place. There, you can buy horses, cows, sheep, chickens, carts, tools, and all kinds of farm products in bulk. Dad sneaks sneaked over to the auction area to restock the farm. I like hearing the fast-talking auctioneer sell everything you would need, starting from fifty cents to the wholesale price of the items.

The line started getting shorter and Mom told our customers,

"You all come back now."

For the people we know, Mom and Dad kept a basket set aside because a lot of them are repeat buyers. Others just wanted an apple or an orange to chew on while shopping. Most of them did not even live in town.

They like to put hay down on the market road to keep our boots from getting muddy. After the selling day was over at three P.M., we helped clean the street area by using steel rakes to remove the straw out of the street. Throwing the horse manure out in a bucket from the vending shack, we were all ready to head home at about four forty-five P.M. Dad unblocked the cart and we headed out to go home after a long day's work. I sat in the back of the cart lying in empty baskets as Dad steered the cart. Mom and Poly sat upfront on the long bench. Chip, Chaney, and Susan decided to stay in town with their friends. As we traveled down the road for the fourth time today noticing the people traveling into to town to gamble tonight, we just missed the incoming traffic, Dad and Mom waving to the passers as we finally got home. With a big grin, Dad said, "go on and let the dogs in, Chris." then I hopped off of the slow-moving cart, ran to the front door, and told both of the dogs to go inside. I threw them some beef chew we had in the pantry and took off my work boots. Mom came in through the pantry door and started up a fire in the kitchen. She put on some bean soup. Dad stayed outside, smoking his pipe next to the outhouse we had moved out into the yard. As he walked in, you could still see the gray smoke rising from the top of the trees like it was a little winter house with a puff cloud over it. I ran outside to the edge line and relieved myself. Then ran back, slowing down to walk pass the outhouse to wash my hands in the soap bucket. As I came inside, Poly was looking around in her high chair as Mom put some day-old bread out and had three bowls of soup on the table steaming hot. I then saw Dad come in while I was in the sitting room.

"Christopher!" Dad yelped, "Come on and eat!"

I walked into the kitchen, sat down next to the steaming hot soup, and ate with Dad, Mom, and Poly as Mom and Dad talked about the boy that got caught fighting earlier today.

Dad said, "What was that boy's name?"

Mom answered, "Which one?"

"The one that got caught stealing goods," Dad said.

Mom responded with "I have not ever seen him in town before today, honey."

As they spoke, my attention span grew weak. It all started to sound like a country singer with a bad voice mumble mumble this, and mutter mutter that.

I downed my soup and went into the study to read the drawing book that Chaney had gotten from his friend, Sam. It had drawings of every town in America, then little subheading explaining what made the town so great. Like, New Orleans, Louisiana, the Marti Gras city. You could see drawings of people having a party in the streets. Mom went upstairs to put Poly to bed. Dad sat on the porch with his newspaper he had brought in town. Leaving out from the pantry door, I needed to get clean. I went to the outhouse then came inside and got ready for bed.

My mom specialized in a whole lot of things; one of her main hobbies was keeping the garden lot. Right out back, you could get the best tomatoes, lettuce, spices, watermelon, and celery. She kept everything you needed to cook within her garden. You could sit out there and eat for days in her lot. Dad made Mom move most of her garden across the road to the small vegetable lot. He said he was running out of standing area for his smoke. Mom kept turnips and potato patches in her lot. Many people liked to buy from her stand during the weekend market. She had a large variety of fruits and vegetables ready for each week. The local store only liked to buy in bulk, so Mom sold it all at her own stand at the market on the weekend. Chip and Chaney liked to pull the vegetables up and eat them during the day. Every time Mom found something missing, we all blamed it on the ground hog that no one could ever find. Mom brought in the vegetables and pickled them for winter using cucumber juice and apple vinegar, bottling them in Mason jars. I like to drink out of the Mason jars because the lid keeps bugs out while we played in the field. Mom keeps a whole pantry stocked full of glass goods in shed two over by the main barn. I maintain the same glass and put just about anything Mom juices in it.

Susan and I helped Mom with churning butter. The process takes forever. The butter churner is made from liquor barrels that Dad had gotten from the Jack Daniels plant in Nashville. Chaney used the corkscrew drill to make a hole in the top, and we put a raft ore in the middle of the churn to bat the curd skim into butter. You could use the same process and make some good cheese. Dad is particular about his fungi collection and he never lets us touch it. The jars that he keeps his cheese fungi in are inside the upper barn and are made with a wooden top to them screwed tight. If you had a coin, you could rub some of that stuff on the coin and then throw it into the barrel. After about three to four months, you would have the best cheese you have ever tasted.

We have steer and milking cows in the side barn area. They like to forage around the barn area and eat away the grass. When Chip or Chaney do not rustle the cows to a new staging area, Dad complains. The reason why Dad complains about the cows is that it keeps the grass even around the barn. We have to heat the milk to boiling every time before selling it to the market, this process takes place every Friday. We use the pasteurization house to heat the boggle pan. After heating the milk to boiling, we separate the milk, curd, and skim. Then stick the milk, curd, and skim into the icehouse for storage. On Monday, Dad and Chip take two carts full-hauled of milk into town with two blocks of ice for the market store on Main Street.

~Chapter 9~
The Wolf

The Wolf

I did not like it much when the class appointed me as one of two teacher helpers. Every week, the class votes on who they want to appoint as the two new teacher helpers. Miss Parity sent around little slips of paper the attendees wrote their nomination down just like an election ballot. They all wrote three names on the piece of paper from one row in the class. This way, the same person is never chosen twice. This week, it happened to be the fourth row's turn for teacher helper; that is the nine, ten, and eleven-year-old row.

"Class," Miss Parity said, and everyone started passing the pieces of paper up to the front, "who are the lucky two this week?" Miss Parity finished her sentence. Chaney had a smirk on his face as if to say, *We fixed this election outside*. Then he nodded and pointed at me. There happened to be more older children in class than younger. It just happened that this year was the first year that they combined the two schoolhouses together to move a couple of the children from the city area because a little bit too much was going on in town. They had the Catholic Boarding School children at our school temporarily while the war was going on, just to keep the children safe from being involved in the fighting. The fact that the children were carted out to Sycamore every day by Father McEgret made a big difference from a twenty-person schoolhouse to a forty or so schoolhouse every other day you see the Pasture Father McEgret or a boarding home director come out to make sure everything is running smooth. By the end of the election, the class chose an older girl named Ann and me as teacher helpers for the week.

My friend, Peter, had to make fun of me. He said, "Nothing's worst than being the teacher's pet." A month ago, my dad started making me wear Benjamin Franklins. He said it made me look well studied. They were originally made for Chaney he never liked wearing anything on his face. It bothered him after a while; he ended up with large red scratch marks on his face from the irritation of wearing face glass. His motto was, "If I can throw straight, I do not need Ben Franklins." Peter said it and he said it again: "Christopher's a teacher's pet, Christopher is a teacher's pet!"

I told him, "You take that back now!"

One of the big kids said, "We are just funning with you."

No, I did not like it and my sister Susan tried to make me feel better by telling me she had been looking for a man with puddle glass on his face to date. That way, Dad could not hit him. This even made it worst. I was expected to do the smart man's job because I wore smart man's glasses; if you look the roll, then play it. What the rule is, Benjamin Franklins are so hard to make; nobody is allowed to lay a hand on the person wearing them. If they want to fight, they would have to ask you to remove your Benjamin Franklins.

Another item Dad wants us to wear was a bow tie. Bow ties fell like someone has got a choke hold on you all day long. Chaney and I always took ours off as soon as we got up the road a little bit. It went into our change pocket in the inseam of our pants. Then when we got out of school, we stuck it back on while closing in on the house so Dad will not notice it missing. Bow ties are for people that have big chicken gizzards in their throat; it makes them look more educated.

Chip said, "What are you doing holding on your neck, because your head might fall of?"

"No," I answered,

"Dad made us wear these black bow ties to school."

Chaney had the straight face Chip liked to make fun on us about school because he already graduated. Every time I would wear a bow tie, I looked like a clown at the circus show. The tie would never fit; plus, big ears and ties do not mix. It would tie up then I would walk around looking like a Dutch playwright. The Benjamin Franklins hid my face and made my eyes poke out like a dragonfly.

There was a story going around town about General Ulysses S. Grant: That the confederate did not know that he was the commander and cut his head off during the battle of Gettysburg. They said he rode around with his head underneath his arm before putting it back on and riding on to meet Stonewall Jackson on the hill. The people in this town are always telling stories to make war generals look like imaginary characters in one of those superhero books. General Grant came down the Tennessee River and took Fort Henry with his broadside battleship and every since then they have been making stories up about him at school. Chip said if you believe that story, you have to be one stupid wood chuck.

Miss Parity had Ann and another girl organizing books on the shelf all day Tuesday and it was not even a school day. Every once in a while a B got where an E would go and an O and Q would get mixed up. All in all, I think we did a good job. Ann had to correct me about the H coming before the P so I had to look at my alphabet practice to see what went where. After cleaning this morning, Miss Parity let us go home and eat. We had to be back at the schoolhouse by two o'clock to complete the next tasks. Ann took off like a bat out of hell and I went the opposite direction to get home by twelve o'clock just in time to see my brothers, Chip and Chaney, play with Dad's new bull. One of the town's boys Jesse was over and they were funning with the bull at the ranch section of our farm.

"Let us see how fast this one is," Jesse said.

"Well, now he is just a little bullet not anything to be scared of, huh," Chaney responded.

I saw Susan dumping water out the door from the corner of my eye and she shook her head as if she was displeased with my brother taunting this bull. Our two oxen moved to the other pen away from the new bull, so Dad had locked them in the side gate over by the bull pen's entrance.

"We have to know how big it will get," Chaney said to Jesse. Then I asked Chip if he could ride the bull.

Right then, I heard the little voice of Poly yelling that lunch was ready underneath my mom's larger voice. It was exactly twelve o'clock. At the same time, Chaney said, "What you know about bull riding, Chris?"

Chip said, "Last one back is a rotten egg!" and we all took off running to the house to get lunch. Chaney was the fastest. Chip keep up and of course, my little feet and breathing condition could not keep up with Chaney nor Chip.

Jesse started his way home, even though he was always invited to eat. Jesse had a funny way about him, almost like he did not like my Mom's cooking or something. When we got in, Susan and Dad were already sitting down and Mom came out with a serving tray of long bread full of thin cut meat.

We sat to eat. First, Dad said grace. He always went on about keeping the family safe from danger, then plentiful food, then last, for his wonderful children and beautiful wife. I weased a little through the whole blessing. Susan asked for the juice. "Pass me the berry juice, please."

"Carl, you not see Chris does not have too much air," Chaney said while passing the berries to Mom. Then Mom passing passed the juice to Susan. Mom and Susan liked to squish berries, making juice from different types of fruit. Every other juice tasted different. The juice was finally passed to me. Susan poured it out; I drank it down fast and had a blue ring around my mouth. Mom looked over and patted her lip with her napkin as if to say, I had to do the same in order to clean my mouth, so I looked at Mom raise her right arm then I wiped my mouth with my sleeve.

Dad said, "No matter what kind of schooling these boys have, they still act like boys, uncivilized with no table manners."

Mom answered Dad with, "I raise gentlemen not slobs."

"You heard your Mom," Dad said."

"Yes, Ma'am," I answered.

"Use your napkin next time," Mom said.
Dad and Chip were smiling while Chaney and I shoveled the meat sandwiches in our mouths. I noticed Poly had a little pie of diced meat in front of her and some peas she was working on. Susan with

her legs crossed under the table and a napkin in her lap was the only one other than Mom that ate like a civilized human. All the rest of us chugged down juice and bit at the ends of the sandwiches like savage beast that had not eaten in years.

After eating lunch, I put my dishes in the kitchen wash bucket and I took off running back to the schoolhouse. Almost tripping on myself and seeing Mr. Riley walking a hag back toward his property, I just waved hi to him and kept trying to move my feet as fast as they could maneuver. The sky was blue with the warm sun just overhead and two clouds that looked like the wind was smoking a cigar. The birds were chirping loud as I went on. I could see the black squirrel poking his head in and out of his den. When I had gotten to school, my teacher Miss. Parity and Ann were already talking outside.

"Fifteen minutes early," Miss Parity said.

I was thinking about Dad's term crap always rolls downhill." He would put a pile of it on top of the hill by staging area two and then when it rained, it pushed the dung down the hill. Two months later, we would plant the hill, the side hill would grow faster than the field. I was only a couple of minutes late, *but to womenfolk, that is an eternity.*

We then finished cleaning up the schoolhouse placing the little quiz cards back in order one box at a time. Miss Parity while sitting at the large teacher desk said, "Please put the alphabet banner over the board for everyone to read. Yes maim, I answered and went out to get the ladder stole because I was too short to reach all the way up to the eight foot height that Miss Parity wanted the banner to hang over the chalkboard. I knew Ann was not going to give me a boost it just is not lady like. If Susan were here that

86

old alphabet cut out would be up with no problem. Ann's father looked in the door with his big face under the smaller cowboy hat and said

"Hi Ma'am, I am Ann's father, Perry Black; she needs to be home before dark for supper."
Miss Parity said while making sure Mr. Black heard her in a load voice, "After both of you get done, you can both go home." We nodded our heads and posted the banner just like teacher said. Then we both exited out of the schoolhouse. It was about four thirty, Ann's father grabbed Ann's books heading towards the road Dad had sent Chip to get me We met up halfway down the road. I could see Chips long stride from the top of the hill outside the schoolhouse. Chip said "Serves you right being that kiss up with the glasses and tie looking like a maintenance engineer or something."

We walked the dusty road home as Ann disappeared going the opposite direction up at the top of the hill you could see her father and her walking along. As we walked back home Peter and his sister Sandra were outside riding their dads three wheeled bicycle back and forth on the graveled path next to the road. We stopped for a little while to see how this bicycle thing worked. Chip said, "Dad should buy one of these contraptions." The men liked to show them off in town, they would sit up straight and look dignified riding the bicycle through the street, then put it on the horse cart and take it home. It was a new concept that everyone had not yet accepted yet. I did not even ask to ride, it looked too big for me to handle Peter could barely get his feet to reach the pedals. As Sandra was coasting him along, holding the bike up Peters feet would slide off the pedal every other turn.

Chip looked like he did not want to be bothered with the whole task of looking stupid falling off of a bicycle because he has never ridden a bicycle before. This was the big brother syndrome never look stupid in front of little brother. Sandra asked Chip, "Do you want to ride?" Chip answered, "No, I do not want to damage your father's bicycle it must have cost him a lot of something" Mr. Peters liked to try new things then force others to be like him. Mr. Peters came walking up Hello Mr. Peters Chip and I said. Then Mr. Peters said,

" have you boys ever ridden one of these." I said "no" Chip said, "I saw one at the Davison store in Nashville." Mr. Peters responded, "That is where I bought this bicycle from, they had brought it to the county auction and I bided twice just to see how it works. No one in my family has ever ridden such a thing, so I let the children play with it, maybe they can teach me a thing or two about how to ride." Mr. Peters really wanted to see Chip riding the bicycle. He told Peter to get off and let Chip ride "go on and let Mr. Chip ride" Mr. Peters said then Sandra handed the bicycle to Chip and he pedaled it up the drive skirt and back. Not turning well and looking like a wet dog shaking dry Chip handed the bicycle back to Mr. Peters. "Thank you for the ride" Chip said. Mr. Peters responded, "it is a pleasure, tell Henry to come by and try this thing out." "Okay Mr. Peters," waving good bye and starting to walk away Chip had a big grin on his face. He is one of those that never liked to be embarrassed this time his scared caught the eye of Mr. Peter's daughter, Sandra she ran in because they always respected Chip as being this big tough protector. Mr. Peters was a happy go lucky guy and messed up Chips image with Sandra.

We walked on and Chip said, "That thing is not easy to pedal, muscles do not work that way."

I started to laugh because Chip does a lot of clowning around with Chaney and I. He always had a knack of looking good around the ladies every time he would see a dame whether she was young or old he straighten up looking like a gentleman, this is what Mom taught us, it is proper too always look good around women.

Chip said, "I hope I did not embarrass myself in front of Sandra."

I laughed again, Chip started to chase me a little walking on the other side of the road Chip gave me a couple of muscle flinches and said "come over here and walk with me Chris." I came over on Chips side of the road he rustled my hair up then told me "do not tell anybody about the scardy cat on the bicycle, ok." I nodded and we were home before I knew it entering the door, the sun was shading outside. Susan was in the study reading a book to Poly, Mom had a pot on waiting for us, and Dad was out back talking to Mr. Riley and Billy.

You cannot push back on wild life too much before it pushes back on you. It seemed that our forest areas grow at a rapid rate if we do not maintain the farm area the weeds, trees, vines, and other growth will overtake the farm. My Dad Mr. Henry used to call it the sea monster effect, once it gets too big you have to abandon ship, this happened when my Father over worked his hands and had to give them some time off to recover from the long summer planting season. Mom helped out by making pantry goods for the winter this made us gain fat and get large over the winter because she liked to bottle all kinds of fruit and vegetables just in case frost set in early. We never went by the farmer's almanac, all we had to do is send Uncle Owen or Grandpa a letter and they would tell us what to look for during the season. Having a farming family is a good thing because they know exactly what to do.

Chaney and Chip set out to burn back some of the brush around the farmland. "See Chris," Chaney said, "you have to take control of the situation like we do, these weeds and brush coming over on our land, we need to push back on it, to show all this gristle whose boss." Susan came walking up and Chip asked "what you doing out here, we are about to get working ," Susan said" Dad said you both are out by staging area three getting ready to make a field so I came along to see some fire." Her friend Mary sat along the fence post both in their brown dresses and white bonnets looking blank at Chip and Chaney as if they had a mission to complete, waiting to see some action. Chips attitude was as if he did not mind them two teenagers looking on, as he started to do his man thing, but Chaney was over with the whole little girl thing and wanted to see some results. "Hand us all those shovels by the standing post Chris," Chaney said with a laud voice, "you want to see some fire Mary then start digging the water trench, what you think the work going to get done by its self." Chaney tried to put Susan and Mary to work in their dress clothes in all. I could see this was not going to happen, he scared Susan and Mary away in a heartbeat then scoffed a laugh when they started to walk away. Susan and her friend disappeared about this time. I could see them from affair heading to the creek because neither of them where wearing overalls and all of us had ours on. Chip said "Susan and Mary done already out grown their britches they look little

90

ladies, this just is not the type of work for little women who are becoming of age for marriage." The overalls were not made for women, they only fit flat chested girls with straight legs, Macys just did not make overalls that fit women very well, too many body parts became unveiled whenever Mom or Susan would wear them. This made Dad get upset and he always sent them inside, dresses made better clothing for women when they got of age, the girls had to stop doing what we called service work just because they did not fit them overalls. Susan tried every style you could think of, long johns with over alls show too much shape, shirt with over alls show to much hip, nothing in work cloths fit them women properly.

"What you looking at, got something for Susan's friend Mary," Chaney told me. "No, but you do," I responded.

Chaney smiled with a half grin then pointed out the area that needed to be dug. Chip told me, "Go fetch water while we dig." I ran down to the third barn shack and grabbed the bucket my daddy kept on each field. He would leave thirty or forty barrels out to catch rainwater that the hands used when the land got dry. I just pulled out a little ten-gallon bucket of water and dragged it across the path area spilling a bit, as I hauled it. When I had gotten back to where Chip and Chaney were with the little tin of water, Chip started laughing while pointing at the pail, "telling Chaney "Look at that," "Do you think this is going to be good enough for this big project Chris" Chip asked I responded" no, but I did what you asked." Chip with his old man walk said, "That is not going to be enough, we need large barrels of water to loosen this earth, I will tell you what. You two stay here and dig and I will go to get two barrels and a can with the horses." Chip knew I was too small to lift heavy barrels but he liked to tell me to do ridiculous stuff any of the away. Like the time he had me with the Mule backhoe while he went inside to get a new pair of gloves the Mule went ever where on the field but straight, he always got a laugh out of it. The hands never thought it was funny they liked to complete their work and do it the correct way. Bill would tell them all "Don't you go on hurting that boy, he is not so large and he stays to study those books." Mr. Riley and Bill liked to ask me to read a manual or two to them so they could get the new types of crops planted properly. Chip always liked teaching me how to do the big work, even though I was not of age to get it done. He always says this will make you stronger. Dad never intended me to be a farmer Dads motto is, farm life is a hard way to live, I work hard so you do not have to, I want something easier for you boys.

" Therefore, Chip took off about this time Mr. Riley came strolling up, "looks like Mr. Henry got you two busy."

Yes, Sir Mr. Riley Chaney and I responded at the same time. Mr. Riley said with a straight face, "your Dad asked me to come out to make sure you do not over work yourselves out here on making this field flat, hear."

Chaney looked up and handed Mr. Riley the shovel Mr. Riley said "now what is an old man going to do with this",
Mr. Riley told Chaney, "come with me, we are going to get some mules, a back hoe, and a harness," before Chaney could respond to Mr. Riley's comment.

Mr. Riley said," Then we can get to working on this field here." "Where is that Chipper at Mr. Riley said

92

again? I answered, "He is away getting the cart and some water," Mr. Riley said, "Chris when he gets back tell him to take the cart and get some axes, we are going to have a four acre field here."

Chip got back with the cart and I told him, "Mr. Riley is working with us now; he needs you to get the axes out of the shed." So Chip smiled and said, "they sure come better with age" meaning the older a person is the more sensible they work. Chaney is with Mr. Riley and they are getting the backhoe right now I explained. Dad walked by showed his face and said, "you got lucky Mr. Riley decided to come down and help," then Dad disappeared with the little bucket in his hand that I brought out. When Mr. Riley and Chaney came back, they started to make a trench around the field with about a ten-foot fire line. The rest of us cut into the trees a bit, so when the fire hit them they would fall down. By the time, we got all the trees with cuts in them it was nighttime and we were all beat so Mr. Riley told us to meet him early in the morning to continue on the field, Chaney and I had to go to school the next day, Chip got stuck making a field with Mr. Riley.

When we got inside Mom had a pot of rock potato stew on and Dad was in the living room reading his fresh newspaper he had kept from the Market Area last Saturday. I fell in the bed dirt and all, and went to sleep. At about twelve o'clock mid night Dad shook me, then I went down stairs with a candle lit night lamp and washed in the cold water that Dad had drawn for me. Susan was spending the time knitting socks. After washing, Susan through the dirty water out and laid the washtub against the outside wall of the front porch to dry. She drug the tub out the front door and tipped it over the steps to pour it out. Mary my sister's friend always went home at night as if Chaney or Chip was coming on to her or something. I put my long johns on and the boots that were on the floor, took the lantern, and headed out to the outhouse to make my business. It was dark, darker than any other night, I heard an owl and then a screech, I ran like a scared man gone crazy to the outhouse and put the lantern up on the hook when I got finished, I then ran inside almost tripping over my own two feet going up the steps. Susan laughed and said, "scared of the dark," I said, "uh hum" and ran up to bed good night Chris I heard as I jumped under the white cover yelling good night back to Susan.

The next morning I raced down stairs where Chip and Chaney were eating, it was about 4:30 am and they had been talking about the new field. I started eating breakfast with the family, a couple of eggs and a piece of wheat bread. While Dad laughed about the field because he said, "you boys did not know where to start or end without Mr. Riley you take heed from Mr. Riley and he will teach you well, older men know how to get work done in an easy fashion you hear boys." I could see it in Chaney eyes under his breath he said, "No old black man bossing me around." Dad took the newspaper he had and smacked Chaney in the mouth with it then he said, "None of that talk is going on here, he is out there to help and that is exactly what he is doing." Chaney started to do his thing with a frown across his face he pushed on the butter dish just enough to make the butter see saw to the opposite end of the dish, almost about to go over the side of the butter dish, the butter then began to travel back to the middle. Dad watching Chaney do his routine looked over at Chaney and said, "Do not

test me boy and do not disrespect your Moms food."
Mom told Chaney to clean the table they always
worked in twos if you got in trouble with Dad you had
to deal with Mom this was the Smith way they both
considered Mr. Riley family, and our family sticks
together.

We were all off to do morning chores, Susan
stayed behind to help Chaney with the dishes. Poly
went to the living room to play with her doll Miss
Nancy and I was out feeding the animals. After
working on the chores for an hour filling the horse
trough and banging the front mats, I went inside, got
my books ready for school, took a swig of milk in my
favorite wooden cup, and then started to school.
Susan and Chaney were right behind me. Mary joined
up and my friends Peter and Sandra joined in about
the same time I saw Chaney's new girlfriend Clair,
she galloped up to walk beside Chaney and the new
kid Rick.

See Clair lived on the farm just below us Mr.
Hancock's farm he has five children Clair is the only
one out of all five that actually goes to school. I talk to
her brother David and we play every once in a while.
For the most part Clair really likes Chaney they both
grew up together when the new children from the City
started attending at Sycamore Clair needed to state
her claim on Chaney because many girls live in the
south especially this being the war time in all, not
many men were left to tend to the farms in the south.
A whole bunch of widows moved into the city because
their husbands left to fight and some of their
husbands never came back they just found it fit to
stay north.

Clair being this Southern bell liked spending time
with Chaney she is a fun person and likes hanging

with Chaney, Susan, and Mary. Chip never minded the Hancock's very much he went down to see what Bradley was doing but most of them liked to hang around with Dad talking about nothing, the whole family acted as if they have been farmers forever. Every time I go over to see David, he is usually found out back practicing his rifling skills. My Dad does not allow me to handle a rife yet; he says I might end up shooting something I cannot bring back. Therefore, I pull my little slingshot and push over a couple of cans when I go over to see David. Mr. and Mrs. Hancock are very nice people Clair acts more like one of us a little liberal, she hangs out at the stream with my sister Susan and bother Chaney. She is not the shy type always funning around. During working season we barely get to see the Hancock's, they ship their goods North to a service contractor named Wells. This meant the whole family had to work harder during planting season to make their quota. When we got to school, we started in on the cleanup picking up thatch wood and sweeping. Then the bell rang, we went in Miss Parity started to go over Wednesdays assignments as I looked out the window wondering what Mr. Riley and Chipper were doing with the new field. Miss Parity was going over, reading subject maters with the older children, whatever that is, I thought in the back of my mind. Then I looked to watch one of the five Mary's walk out of the class room to use the outhouse, when she came back she smelled like a bull pen in the heat of the summer. We all noticed that no one had cleaned the outhouse for a while, Chaney leaned back in his little chair as me and Susan tried to hold our breath as Mary walked by the rest of the class ignored the fact that the outhouse stunk. No one wanted to burn it, burning dun is considered our fathers job. People get used to their own smell until someone tells them that they stink. The schools out houses are over used. We only have two of them for over forty children and too many strays use it as they pass by, it sets in the corner of the play field by the forest.

Chaney whispered to his friend Rick and Rick started to smile. Susan said to me,

"she must be in the middle of minstrel."
I did not know what Susan meant, words like that confuse me, but all Susan had to say is that it is that time of the month and she gets to stay home. I tried it once and Mom laughed at me and said, "are you really not feeling well Chris." Dad almost cried he laughed, laughing so hard, Dad repeated it "it is that time of month" and Mom said, "That only works with women folks." The trials we go through in a nine year olds body. After school was done, we ran down the hill to the field where Mr. Riley, Chip and Dad were working on cutting down trees.

Dad gave Chaney an axe and told him to cut the trees low," These old sycamore trees got good wood," Dad said. Chop, chop, chop, I saw them chopping all the woods down while Mom and her friends looked like old maids walking with washing baskets to the stream to wash dirty clothes. Susan and Mary went with Mary's Mom and their friend Vivian to the creek to help wash. They took the big wicker baskets, a couple bars of soap made from milk, honey, and flowers then dropped the baskets into the running stream water, which they left in the water for about 30 minutes while scrubbing the clothes. After finishing the scrub cycle, they let the clothes sit in the water for another 30 minutes while they talked about all of us at the stream. That is what Chaney said they did, every time too many women get together they all talked about men because Chaney would get the look and smile from Mary as if he had done something wrong. Chaney then knew, he was the main conversation. When Mom got done washing the clothes she then hung them on lines behind the house, we liked to play around in the back of the house Peter and Sandra would come over and play in the maze Mom made with the clothing ropes and hooks. I like to go out there and play hid n go seek until nightfall. I do this every time Mom hangs clothes.

Dad, Mr. Riley and Chip worked on the trees "now do not go too far yonder Mr. Henry we can pull the trees with the mule after getting a couple good slits in with the axe," Mr. Riley said. Dad let off a node and they started into the trees. Sycamore trees are among the taller trees they sit strong as a donkey dug in waiting for water. The Sycamore stood anywhere from eighty feet to one hundred twenty feet tall, the thing about fielding this land were the roots they span out so far that it is easier to burn the field out. When Mr. Riley, Dad, and Chip got finished cutting the trees and storing the lumber by staging area three, the week was finished. We will have to continue working on clearing the field next week.

On Saturday morning, we all got ready to go to the Market place to sell fruit. Mom had some porridge on, when I woke up the sun was just beginning to come up the purple, orange, and blue of the rising sun was just over the horizon. It almost looked like the sun was pushing down on the trees as it had its hand on the treetops making the trees look smaller and the sky larger. I let off a big yawn and proceeded to the barn to fetch a pail to fill with water. Chaney and Susan had already started feeding the horses at the stable.

Dad, Poly and Chip were tight asleep. I could hear Dad snoring down in the hallway upstairs when I first woken up this morning. I then grabbed the soap and proceeded to the well, drew some water to wash up with. There was not much water left in the rain catch that poured off the roof gutter of the barn. Mom said not to use the rainwater for the pour down because it had not rained for several weeks. Therefore, I changed in the rear barn and washed with a pail of water. By the time I had gotten finished Susan and Chaney had went inside to get ready for the market. As I walked over towards the outhouse, I saw that the cows had already been thrown hay and the water troughs were already full, figuring that Susan and Chaney had finished all the chores for the day. This left time for me to play with the roosters. Our roosters were making a heck of a lot of noise cock a doodle doo repeatedly as if they were men that got no attention. No one even gets up when I make noise anymore I could see Boyde our rooster complaining. Opening the chicken coop gate and going in to play with the chickens and the roosters I chased the brown rooster with the checkered collar and picked him up he was the big noisemaker today, finding out that our red rooster Boyde was not hardly making any noise at all. After rubbing his smooth feathers, I let him loose to peck around with the other roosters and hens. At this time, I saw Chip walking into the barn to start putting the fruit baskets into the sales cart. I ran into the barn,

"good morning Chip" I said,

Chip looked up and waved as if he had his tong tied with a rope. Then he picked up an apple and tossed it at me hitting me in the leg "come on and help," Chip said he had slipped his over alls on over his long johns I was dressed already. "Ok" I told Chip, then I walked over to where Chip was and Chip hopped up on the cart "pass the baskets up, while I put them in the cart." I slid the basket full of apples over to the cart and lifted them onto the ledge as Chip stacked them on one another one at time filling the cart with apples oranges and pears. "You sure are slow, slow as malaises" Chip said with a grin. Mom rang the bell for breakfast Chip and I ran to the pantry door trying to trip each other, seeing who would get to the door first as I put my foot in the door Chip stepped on it and slipped in just enough to squeeze past Mom, I ended up behind Mom. Mom twirled around to see who was breathing at her back then she pointed at the bowl in the middle of the table. Dad was already at the table looking over a rain chart with a glass of orange juice and a half-cup of coffee. I never liked porridge very much it would be soft when you started to eat then after about ten minutes it started to become a brick that the spoon had to chop off chunks of as you chewed it down to swallow. Chaney and Susan swung into their chairs, while Dad drew a bar for precipitation for the month in his ledger; I poured some milk on the butter trying to keep my porridge soft. Poly came in with a blank face carrying her doll that had one shoe on nudging Dad Poly said, "put the other one." Dad picked up his spectacles sending Poly to Mom, saying which one you chased off the rain, Chaney's head popped up and said, "we got too many ugly in this town it won't rain on ugly." Mom slicked back her hair as if to say it is not because of me and we laughed about Chaney's comment.

Dad put the almanac and his ledger under the chair as we heard the dogs barking outside on the porch. Blue came inside and ducted under the table, lying on Chips shoes waiting for some food to come down. Chip asked Susan to pass the bread and tore the end off of it and gave it to blue, blue ran out to the porch feeling special. Dad slurped his porridge down with the spoon without making the slurping sound. We all had to blow on the spoon before sticking it in our mouths. After about fifteen minutes, we were all finished eating and tired of hearing Dad and Mom discuss about how the drought weather had made our next-door neighbors the Hancock's well dry up and how they were ciphering the ground to find a new water vein. This process took forever, you had to drive a thirty-foot rod into the ground and listen for streaming water if there was none then you had to drive another one until you found water. Mom boiled two barrels full of drinking water for them yesterday. After eating, we all set out to the barn and loaded the fruit while Mom and Susan packed our lunch as Poly ate the rest of her pour age, the pour age that was left that she did not spill onto her high chair. Poly usually spills most of the porridge onto the floor and high chair. Mom and Susan usually clean the floor before and after every meal. Today is Monday, I was walking to school with Chaney, Susan, Chaney's Girlfriend Clair, Peter, and Sandra. While walking to school Chaney had the baseball and we threw it back and forth seeing who would drop it first. Dad offered us a ride today we had too many friends walking to school with us to fit into the cart.

Clair was on the front porch waiting before we even finished our morning chores, Mom liked to talk to Clair about the dresses they made and new fabrics.

The girls wore the traditional dress for school and on Sunday, the women wore all kinds of colors to church sundresses purple, pink and white dresses that made them look like flowers standing together. The men on the other hand liked to wear black, brown, and dark blue. We can only wear overalls on the farm never outside the farm; this was a big thing for Dad because he considered overalls as being only work clothes. It was uncouth to wear overalls out.

When we arrived at school, the older children had already finished morning chores the front had been picked up and the schoolhouse was already swept. Miss Parity asked Peters Dad to fix the outhouse problem; he chose Chaney, Rick, Marshal, and Paul to help him tilt the outhouse onto his wagon to move it to its new spot. Sitting in class watching the big kids dig two new holes for the out houses made me realize how inattentive people can be. I was board of listening to Miss Parity talk about the difference between an exact number and a rounded number. "Class do you know the difference between a rounded number and an exact number?" Miss Parity went on. Joseph was sitting in the back of the class sleeping with his mathematics book covering his lace. Miss Parity waited for every ones hands to go up, when she did not see the hand she wanted Miss Parity then called on Joseph and his book fell to the ground with a blank face like a person that woke up from bed. Joseph did not know what was going on, he especially did not know what the question was, his eyes blood shot red, we knew it was beginning harvesting season. Miss Parity pointed to the corner and Joseph sat with the dunce cap on looking at the crescent mirror he had a frown on his face that only spoke of boys who get in trouble. Miss Parity went on,

"exact numerals are numbers that have been accounted for. A rounded number is an estimation that you have   made, a qualified guess."
Chip estimated all the time, Dad never liked it because Dad had to have his books exact. If Dads paperwork did not come out right he would take it into Mom and they had a calculation battle that made more paperwork for adjustments than what he started with.

As I looked out the window I could see Rick pointing at a rope to show Mr. Peters what he was talking about, then they grabbed it and started tying the rope to the mid section of the out house in order to pull the outhouse up on to the horse cart. At this time Miss Parity was ready for a break so she made us write a couple of examples in our ledger books. I wrote twelve, then made twelve circles, then wrote teen, and made twelve circles. May made a screeching sound trying to hold back laughter when I looked up I saw the outhouse had fallen off the cart and landed right back into the place it was before they had started to move it, no one was hurt thank God. The funny look on Mr. Peters face was as if he was thinking in his mind that these boys are incapable of doing any manual labor. You could see Chaney moving his head back and forth as if to say no. Then Rick pulled a board from the side of the school and they shoved the outhouse up onto the cart using the board Rick had grabbed. Mr. Peters yelling at the top of his lungs "You boys move out the way!" I had always thought that Mr. Peters was the calm resourceful type. I guess I was wrong or this little bossy guy came out of him when work needed to be done. No matter what the case, it surprised Miss Parity, you could hear him from inside, Miss Parity paused checking the ledger books and dismissed the class to the play yard, everyone except Joseph.

"Class dismissed for mid-daybreak," Miss Parity said in her scratchy something is going wrong voice. Pointing over at Joseph Miss Parity said," you stay there," then she handed him his books to put underneath the chair. After the last child left, Miss Parity decided to talk to Mr. Peters. We all ran outside to play. Susan said, "Awe Mr. Peters must be in trouble with Miss Parity."

As they played chase I could see Chaney's head above the bushes of the new area the outhouse was going to be moved to. Chaney had to take charge of the whole situation of the outhouse movement. I saw Chaney hop into the wagon, Rick and Paul leaning over the back edge of the cart while Marshal guided it on the ground to the area they wanted to place the outhouse. Peter ran over and coasted the outhouse into place helping Rick, then plop went the women's outhouse and they were half way done with the work.

Miss Parity held Mr. Peters up long enough for the boys to get some work done. Now all they had to do was fill in the holes to cover the mess up. These outhouses have not been moved in over a year so they had seven-foot holes full of it just waiting to be covered. After talking to Mr. Peters Miss Parity rang the bell for lunch, we ran over and got our lunch bags Joseph came running out with the dunce hat still on his head to get some lunch as we all ate outside at the picnic tables you could see the older children making fun of Josephs dunce cap. Chaney and crew came back smelling like garbage, the bad smell was in their school clothes as they sat by the tree and ate the bread, jelly and cheese that their moms packed for them.

Sitting down talking to Susan and her friends Sandra and Mary, they were over at the table telling about the dangerous trip Sandra's father Mr. Peters had to make to take package goods to the troops in Southern Virginia. "I am not too interested in that war stuff as long as they have something to fight over they are going to fight" Mary said. "This war is taking away all the marrying men from the town and it seems like they are never coming back home" Susan said. About this time, I lost interest, hearing how the women in town are not being catered to and all made my stomach get sick. This was becoming an old hag conversation quick and I had better things to do. Then I gathered my trash and went to sit next to Peter. Hey, Peter. Hi Chris," what is new Peter?" My father is trying to put together a steam tractor. What is it a train on wheels? If you want to you and Chaney can stop by and look at the tractor run. He got the parts from the Peabody shop over in North Carolina. Aw, we have to finish on the field my father wants it cleared before the end of harvest. Is not that something that you do in the springtime? Peter asked. They need it cleared now to make the field fertile by spring.

Someone had wrapped the bell string around the base of the bell holder on the side of the school. This made it hard for Miss Parity when she went to ring the bell she was unable to reach the cord handle. It had to be a prank from one of the big kids' they liked to play gages whenever someone had a dunce cap on. Miss Parity reached up, when she could not reach the bell rope she then got a stick and rang the bell, we all packet our stuff and ran inside Miss Parity did not say a thing about the bell pulley.

As soon as we sat down Miss Parity said go and get your books off of the shelves and start reading for your next week's assignment, we all moved fast to the bookshelves avoiding a line, I went after Moby Dick again, as the big kids grabbed the newer books on the self. I was not pleased when I ended up with Davy Crockett a Pioneer of Eastern Tennessee. I have only heard stories about him and Daniel Boone. Dad used to refer to him as a politician Dad walked around the house on many of occasions complaining, that Davy Crockett does not know anything about the people's rights that is a crock full of bull. Sitting there reading, the class became quit and Miss Parity sat at her desk with her legs crossed looking over a stack of history papers. Everyone in class had their heads down and every once in a while a hand would go up and ask for a word or two from Miss Parity. If it were a common, word that was hard to pronounce Miss Parity would write it on the chalkboard for everyone to see. Miss Parity putting the words on the board made the older children ask fewer questions because they were embarrassed when she wrote the word on the board. It just plumb made you feel stupid.

After about two hours of reading Miss Parity stood up in front of the class, and said "children, children before you are dismissed for the day remember to do your ten math problems any math you can find around where you live and turn it in on Wednesday. Class dismissed. "We all picked up our sacks and headed out side Chaney, Susan, Peter, Sandra, Clare, and Rick waited outside for me because my bags happened to be at the bottom of the pile. As we headed down the hill one of the Mary's waved good bye and I waved back. Heading home after school Chaney and I knew what Dad had in store for us. We threw the ball back and forth until the picket fence came up with our family name on the entrance sign.

Dad and Chip were out at the field still clearing it while the hands Bill and Mr. Riley were out plowing the fields.

When we entered the door, Mom was sitting in living area knitting. "Hi Mom," I said as I tried to run past to my room when Mom stopped me and said, "You are not going to give your Mom a hug." "All Mom," I said as Chaney did the same thing sneaking behind me and proceeding up the stairs, he made it all clear. As I gave Mom a hug and a kiss, Chaney got pass with no problem. I missed you all while you were at school, we missed you too Susan interrupted just long enough for me to get away and upstairs to change into some work clothes. Poly made her way down stairs looking up at me and pointing as I whizzed past. I slipped on my work shirt and overalls, put my school clothes inside the bed chest and whizzed downstairs where Mom and Susan were knitting. Then Chaney came downstairs, "come on pecker head let us get going," Chaney said and we started to the door. As soon as we got outside, I told Chaney about Peter's Dads steam tractor. "Peter said that his Dad is building one of those new steam tractors," "really" Chaney responded, "yes really," I said. "We have to go over Mr. Peter's house some time and check this out" Chaney answered. By the time, we got to the field Chip had a big grin on his face as if to say we have this all under control. Dad said, "You boys came just in time to see the fireworks." Dad started explaining to Chaney "after putting slices into all of the trees we got a little flag to tell which way the wind was blowing to make sure the fire went toward the fire lines at the end of the field. We used some barrels of water and lined them up on the fire line it took about forty." As Dad explained to

Chaney and I, Chip had his arms folded with the big work gloves on looking like a Forrester at the end of his workday. Nodding his head as if to say we are in control, Dad started to pour out some oil mixed with sulfur and then said stand back boys. He lit the fire and the fire burned in the middle of the trees, grass, and leaves.

Dad ran to the side of the field where we had the fire trench, it had some stand still ready water in it from the irrigation that Chip, Dad and Mr. Riley built earlier this morning. Come on lets go inside nothing to see out here. Just as the fire started to become hot, we heard a cry then a wolf came running out of the area with a rabbit in his mouth. Chaney did you see that wolf? Chaney smiled, "looks like someone needs to find a new home." Dad said, "He must have got in there when we broke for lunch," as we walked off the smoke filled air looked dusty and black. We had enough firewood to last two years piled up by shed one. As Dad, Chip, Chaney and I walked away, we knew our work was closes to being completed.

Walking along the path looking back in intervals to see the gray smoke rise up as the wind carried off the forestry smoke, I had never seen a controlled fire before this amazed me. When we got to the house, Susan was on the porch looking at the smoke as if it was an Indian symbol to beware. Chaney with a big grin, Dad with a chuckle, and Chip with a laugh all nodded over at Susan as Poly pointed at the mushroom in the sky
"say fur, fur ,"

Poly said. We walked inside and Mom said done with the field clearing, Dad chuckled and told Mom about the brush fire that we had just lit." We had to light it up, be careful around staging area four, the fire is going well out there," Dad explained to Morn. The farm filled with the smell of ash Chip started out to the pasture area to bring the cows into the barn. Come on boys we got some animal wrestling to do. Chaney and I followed Chip out to the fenced area behind the barn and we showed the cows into the barn and gated them in for the night. Ya ya get in there!! "Go ahead Chaney lock em in," Chip said in his western voice. "Got cha Chip," Chaney responded as the gates closed and the chained pins fell into place I could hear the mowing of the cows. I told Chip, "they must have been scared stiff from all that smoke." Chip gave a node as Chaney got the last pin in. Then we headed to the porch where Dad was adding to the smoke with his pipe "Yep you boys get some study in, change out of those dirt filled cloths." Bob and Mr. Riley danced around the corner looking upward at the sky. The next morning the fire was smoldering out. Besides a couple of trees and a stone or two that needed to be moved the land looked just about ready to be loosened. The ground was as black as night and the soil as dark as coffee Dad was proud of his boys for making the field Mr. Riley really knew a whole lot about cropping. His expertise made it easier for us to make the field. Then the next week Bill and Mr. Riley took an ox and two horses and tended the field.

~Chapter 10~
Off Hunting

Off Hunting

Every year around November Dad, Chip, and Chaney go off to Uncle Owens hut in the Blue Ridge Mountains to meet up with Uncle Nick and Grandpa. I always wanted to go but Mom said I was too small and she wanted me to stay home while they went off. There is not much to do on a farm during the wintertime you still have to feed the animals and go pull stock from the grain silo Dad, Chip and Chaney secured the farm before they left. I did not like hanging around with my older sister Susan or my younger sister Poly, Peter, and me went out to play. Mom sat back in her rocking chair knitted and drew new knitting patterns on paper. We have plenty of food there is always something in the oven during the wintertime Moms over cooking keeps the house warm.

Susan and Mom looked a lot alike, kind of like identical twins the more they hung out together the more and more alike they seemed to look, my friends could barely tell them apart the differences between the two was slim pickings. They both had red hair from the Scottish part of my family. My Grandpa called it, "A family of nothing but Farmers and Peace keepers," Grandpa would say," it is nice to see Nick own his shop." During the wintertime Peter, David and I would go back and forth to each other's property and always end up at some of the sycamore trees down by the creek playing with the girls in the area. Tag or hide n go seek sometimes making little wooden boats and floating them down the creek while running along with them. Other times we would walk our dogs and then when it snowed ride sleighs down the long gradual sloping hills. Throw rocks at wooden posted tree targets that my brothers made for shooting practice or knocking over bottles that we set up on the fence posts. Sitting in the swing at school or the one Dad made from an buggy wheel a rope knotted in the middle dangling from the Henry Oak tree, using the sliding board at school riding up and down on the teeter-totter.

No matter what, there was always something to do. Even if we stayed inside and played with our Christmas toys until nightfall, it was something. I have a little handmade town and some carved people with dress clothes on, Poly likes to run away with the toys and play with them by herself. We have got to teach Poly how to share. If all and all was right Peter and I would throw the ball back and forth until our hands froze and then we go inside to warm up. Mom," I am going over Peters to play." "Ok, be back by supper." Then I left to walk the hill to Peter's house. I traveled up the hill and through the long driveway of woods in order to get to Peters two story country house. Dave our next-door neighbor never came over to my house he always stayed at home with his family. He and Peter liked to hang out, my guess is that the Hancock's like to keep a close eye on their children. I knocked on the door then sat on the porch Peter's Mom came out and said they were a half mile out in the wooded area working on clearing a path for a rail system that Peter's Dad needed for his distillery." Come in until they get back Christopher," Peters Mom said. I waited for an hour after being invited in talking to Sandra as she combed her dolls hair, while eating up the cookies that Peter's Mom sat in front of me.

113

Peter's Dad had a good amount of land and left it mostly forest. Mr. Peter likes the simple life. He owned a large distillery in the back woods on his property; he had hired two local men to help him make harps Mr. Mike Gobs and Mr. Joseph Kleeper. They had to haul the barrels into town keeping the bars going twenty-four seven. Mr. Peter knew how to live. He is the life of any party talking about every other new invention known to man. Mr. Peter is always working on some new industrial feat. This type invention go-getter only liked to mess with inventions that where proven to work. Peter and I built a fort in his father's woods we made it nice. With an upstairs and a down stairs, a tree house may be what you might call it. The tree house was about a quarter mile away from Peter's house in the backwoods of his father's place. It is built on the side of a blue spruce about sixteen feet straight up and two stories to it, that made the whole tree house look nice, it has an upstairs with a look out area and a down stairs with a room for hanging in. We have plenty of head space Peter's father helped us with building the tree house by supplying the wood and showing us how to build a tree house from the ground up. See Peter and I went about building the tree house in three stages. First stage was to make a stable platform in the tree that is built nice and even this allows use to play marbles on the floor. After making a twist tie rope latter to climb up in to the tree Peter's father cut a couple of branches to make it easier for us to build the platform for the tree house. Next, we nailed 4x4 boards in to the tree with 10-inch stake nails. Building a square around the tree it provided the main platform for standing on then doing the same thing 10 feet up made us a new roof. After including 2 x 4 cross boards that spiraled out like an umbrella. Our 2 x 4 boards that went out at an angle and then a median and another median at the ends making the whole tree house look like a big octagon building. We built the roofed area the same way, we cut some sheet wood to build the outer walls like a big C on the far side of tree house, the wide-open space provided a comfortable living area. When we got finished building the tree house, it looked like a hunters post. While looking down onto the forest our tree house made a nice place for us to see just how brilliant the colors of a wooded area are. We could see as far as the eye could see over some of the smaller trees and directly into the larger Sycamore trees.

I was explaining to Sandra about the difference between the bobcat and the lynx. "So what are you and Peter planning to do today?" Sandra asked. Well I responded, we are going to go and play out in the woods today. Sandra looked puzzled as if to say you play in the woods every day, a simple answer to a simple question. Peter came running up and asked me if I had had anything to drink, "Christopher did you get anything to drink" his mother placed a cup of milk in front of me and I drank it down, "Thank you Mrs. Peter I responded." Mrs. Peter nodded and went back into the kitchen. Peter's Dad was still down in the woods telling the crew how he wanted his track laid. Peter said "guess you were waiting a good while" I said "yes" while sucking down the milk trying to keep from a spill, then pausing enough to utter a couple more words, "just watching your sister Sandra comb her dolls hair." Peter ate up some cookies and then chugged the milk down heading toward the door Peter said," Let's go." Then we both left out the door and ran down the hill to the bypass by the little creek turning right then left and then right again. Before I knew it, we were right there, standing in front of Mr. Peter while he was getting the fellows to lift the iron tracks to place them. They were out in the woods cutting trees and driving stakes into the 8 x 12 inch wood running along the ground with rails lined along the wood and a man with black jack gloves and face shield welding the tracks together for Peters Dad. "Hi Mr. Peter," I said he looked down and told Peter ,"stand back from a safe distance and watch, this type of work could be dangerous son," in a stern voice "stand over by that elm tree and look" Mr. Peter barked again. We both ran over to the elm and watched as Mr. Peter, Mr. Gobs, and Mr. Kleeper all worked on digging a smooth platform for the boiler pull train. They had contracted a lift made of a rope pulley made for the farm hay pull up plank and stuck it in the back of a mule cart. Using two horses to pull the metal along the tracked area as the metal slid on the ground until it got to its destination and then they proceeded to drop the iron track in place on top of the boards located in the dug earth. Mr. Kleeper sounded," Ya, ya horse move that wood on." The horses moved and then they stopped Mr. Gobs ran over and then slipped the half tied knot loose, with a big clank you could hear the iron hit and bounce up and down off of the wood smashing down the dirt making dust fly into the air.

Peter and I looked for a good thirty minutes then ran down to the creek to play. After about an hour, we heard a large clapping noise coming from the area that Peter's father was working on. Then another clapping noise, this one even louder than the first one. Chuck chunk chuck chunk were the next sounds we heard as we splashed rocks in creek Peter then said,

116

"Let us go back and find out what is going on with the train." I agreed, "Come on Peter," we were ready to go back to the work site in order to see what the noise was.

As Peter and I took off running getting closer and closer to the work site, a tall thin man with a scrappy beard and u shaped bald started to come into view. He was standing in front of a little cart with a boiler on it and two pull rods. The wooden cart moved along the ground slowly toward the track, then lined up on the track with his tall lanky body swaying back and forth, as the man pulled out his gadgetry and tools to measure the distance between the cart wheels and the train track. This was the very first train I had ever seen that actually functioned properly. I have seen teeter-totter track movers but never an actual train. It stood lower than a horse but made more noise than a chicken on a hot plate. "Stand back boys and let Mr. Orval do his thing," Mr. Gobs said. Clap and then sparks flew from the front two wheels. Mr. Orval hoped off the train and then called out,

"you need to level the track out a little."
Mr. Peter frowned and then all of them broke for the house, while Peter and I ran over to the clubhouse to look down on the train I had never seen such a thing it was surprising that with so much coiled metal that this contraction actually worked. It started to overcast dark and the whistle of the night creatures was beginning to be heard all over the frosty air by the time Peter's Dad and Mr. Orval came back down with Mr. Gobs and Mr. Kleeper it was ready for nightfall. Peter and I were up in the tree talking about school reading, a book of space creatures called Sand Man and then pitching marbles across the floor to see who could knock the others out of the ring.

I got down as soon as Mr. Orval and Mr. Peters walked out to the train with an unlit oil lamp. "Hay Peter it is time for me go home before my Mom comes looking for me." I waved good-bye and took off with a fast walk down to the road past Peter's house and to the main road, it took about thirty minutes to get home by the time I entered the gate it was dark. Mom was working in the kitchen on a rooster for dinner and Susan must have been down at the other farm hanging with her friend Mary. I went into the front room to play with Poly and saw that Poly was busy building herself a wall out of letter blocks. In I came and started to build my own wall occasionally Poly would take one of my blocks and add it to her wall, this went on until I had two blocks left and Poly had a perfect wall. "Mom Poly is stealing blocks from me," I said. Moms head entered the room, "play with something else Christopher." "She is not sharing Mom," I said again. Then Mom laughed because Dad liked to do things on his own just like Poly. Susan and Mary came in the door and then I went to the outhouse to get clean as I passed by Susan glanced and said that is my shy brother. Mary laughed and I said, "nun hum." Headed to the palace and then left out by the chicken coop to see which cock Mom snagged for dinner. I saw gray and red but milky was missing, this was the one we were eating. Milky had a personality to himself. He would walk around showing off his feathers as if to say he was better than all the rest of the chickens and never made a nestling with a hen, too good for the hen's Dad said this one might be sick, I would not put my luck in Milky. We never saw a hatchling look like old Milky.

I walked in and then sat down to say grace. Mom, Susan, Poly, and I were at the dinner table; Mary had left just as she did every other evening. As we sat down, I noticed that Poly was actually at the table and not in her high chair located in the breeze area of the dining room. "Wow, is Poly old enough to sit at the table." Mom looked over and said" I do not see why not." I have to get your father to build a longer table to seat everyone Susan interrupted, "Chip or Chaney may move out and find themselves a little sweet heart." Mom responded,

"Do not be talking about them like that."
 Mom could not stand to see one of the boys move away, she is so settled into the way our family is, that change is not in her mind right now.

Christopher would you do the honors, then I started on my grace that asked for forgiveness for sin, then well to do food, last the family health. After finishing, the grace we all sat quit for a minute. Then I broke the ice by asking, "Susan please pass the gravy." It started the slow journey down Susan's side of the table to Mom and then Poly but Poly only sat and looked at the gravy bowl as it sat in front of Poly I realized that having a little girl at the table might hinder the passing of food. As Poly looked around then pointed at the gravy bowl I then had to perform Dads biggest no no. Never get up from the table without first excusing yourself. "Excuse me as I get the gravy" Mom and Susan had smirks on their faces as I rowed down the table and graved the gravy for my plate of chicken. Then in one straight movement got back to my seat and pulled my seat in. Mom, "everything is well." "You might want to get your fixings before you sit down Chris" Susan said, I looked up and noticed that Mom and Susan already had everything they needed on their plates. I was the only one that had to run around the table to get my plate full. I then decided to settle for chicken with gravy and a salad with no dressing on it this way I would not have to get any other fixings. Susan grabbed my plate and then served me a little of everything on the table looking as if to say, he is only a nine year old. Mom ran to the kitchen, got the pitcher of orange juice, and poured some after wards my plate was filled well with plenty of food on it. Mom said, "Now stop eyeing your food and eat." I said "Thank you Susan for fixing my plate" Susan responded "anything for my helpless little brother, that has to do everything the hard way." After dinner, I went into the study and collected up all of my toys to put them on the wall properly.

~Chapter 11~
Playing with Toys

Playing with Toys

It seemed we had every other toy you could think of in the toy room past the study. Mom and Dad had plenty of stuff on the top shelves of the toy room that they did not want anyone to play with. Susan had her Lazy Sue doll that she kept on the top shelf. The eyes would close when the doll was laid down; it had a purple and black dress that made it unique. Dad had a little water well and pump that he kept in the study. The cart that carried a barrel with a see saw and a hitch latch that was all made of wood was one of my father Volunteer Fire Department trinkets. Chip had his Horse set with the little man on top of the Wagon every time it would go forward the little mans wipe would fly through the air and then back again. Mom had herself a ballerina that played music and twirled around as it went in a circle playing the dancing music. Now Dad kept a guitar in the study while my little people set with wooden buildings sat inside of a wooden box marked city the guitar sat on top of it. Poly had taken over all of the stuffed toys such as the stuffed sea otter that Granddad bought and the red headed patch dolls that came from New York Granddad had brought a whole lot of toys for us, Christmas two years ago. Dad liked to keep it to birthdays and holidays that is the only time we would get toys from Dad. Such toys like the Russian Matryoshka doll or Nestling Dolls in the study room. Toys like the Wilson fire cart and the stuffed pincushions Mom made, time and time again for her sowing, she had collection of great toy animals to play with. We also have porcelain dolls that my Mother bought from a Chinese guy in town one week end. See toys are very important to children we like to have something to do on cold wet rainy days playing in the toy room is the best way to stay out of Mom and Dad's way. When Mom or Dad catch us moping around they make us clean the house and that is not fun at all. I make tents with some of the bed sheets, blankets in the, and use a storage box or two to block off a compartment that will allow me be able to have rooms inside the tent.

It all works well until Chip or Chaney come in and start doing their under construction routine. "Your tent is under construction," Chaney would say then he would rip a part of it down and tell me I need to rebuild. This worked well for Chaney because if Poly or I told on him we would have to rip down the whole tent then Dad would come in and tell us to move it outside," The house is no place to build tents" Dad says, Puppets are all ways a treat to play with as long as my brothers do not make them act like poor greedy people or immigrants that just came off the boat at Ellis Island. Chip and Chaney liked to get laughs out of our toys. The two stringed puppets that we had one of them Victorian Queen Ann and the other one an black Dock Worker with a blue and white Navy suit on made some fun for us having the one red head talk to the Navy. My Dad had a rocking horse with a straw tail and Poly's rocking crib. Playing with toys helped us pass the time away. If there is time to be spent we set up a tea party for Poly including all of her favorite toys. Then we could introduce the friends as they passed teacups around the room. This was the only play area we had, the minute the room got junky Dad or Mom would kick us outside. Susan did not like playing with the toys in the toy room she would rather sit and knit just like Mom. Susan gives a laugh or a smirk, especially when Chip or Chaney started doing their thing with the string puppets. The black Dock Worker always tried to get fresh with the Queen and end up getting him-self in a world of trouble. It was funny at first but then it got dull. We tried to get Susan and Mom to make some new clothes for the puppets so we could make up new skits but Mom put the puppets inside a glass container and locked them so no one could play with them she said," We were uncouth with the puppets." The big rocking horse that stays in the corner never gets played with because it is too small for us big kids and too hard to hold onto by the little ones so it never gets used not unless you have a super strong child that is two or three years old that is able to hold onto the rocking horse. That is the only way it will ever get used. I think I heard Dad talk about Chip riding the rocking horse but Chip was a born steer rider any of the way. All of us just fell off of the dog gone horse. The sea horse lined box that we store our little toys in makes for a nice place to display our wooden collection of little work horses and carriages. The funny thing about it is whenever Dad or Mom sees us playing in the toy room they send us to the study to work on studying our bookwork. Then we all give an awe and go into the study that is the next room over and pick up a book or two to read.

Planting fields can be a long tedious job. First, you have to wait until after the initial spring rain. It usually happens around the middle of April. This rain brings plenty of water that moistened the ground loosening it for planting. Then we till the land, depending on how large your field is a Farmer may need a back hoe or a Whitney to make the planting rows. Most fields

125

consist of rows of close to one hundred square of any crop you can think of until the land is full; a hundred takes about two to three acres of land. To till the land you need a couple of good oxen that can pull a the large ten foot back hoe this is a big blade that we use to make planting areas, it cuts into the dirt and makes nice rows that you can plant seed into. When the soil is up into a peek at the top or in the valley of the peek is where you want to plant seeds depending on what you are planting. Hand planting is hard most of the time we can use a bullhorn or an ureter pole to place seeds or beans in the ground. When planting seeds that way you do not have to keep bending down to plant your crop. After using the bullhorn for the whole ten acres of land, you will use a roller and two horses or oxen to pull the roller over the seeds to make sure they are in the ground. Then we bring a cart full of barrels of water and use a large pot to dump water all over the crop from the back of the cart. If you do a good job, the soil will not dry out. Some irrigation is needed to make sure moister does not leave the field, in-between the rows there are usually little debits that trap excess water. We then irrigate around the field to channel the water where you need it. Making a large channel from our gully, lake, stream or creek this insures we have a good amount of water to allow the crops to grow. Every field should have a well dug, every once in a blue moon the wells go dry so you might have to go to the stream to get more water to pan the field. It helps to build a water wheel to pump water from the ground up to the area you need to be irrigated.

When it comes to planting stuff Dad usually calls on Chip, Chaney and Mr. Riley, we just got two new Work Managers Mr. Smith and Doug. Doug is not too smart but he gets the job done. Once Dad sent him for chicken wire and he came back with a live chicken, Chaney and his smart ways," I hate to tell you Doug but we are at a wheat field not at the chicken coop." Doug was embarrassed; I guess this is what happens when you do not listen fully to what people say. Dad said Mr. Smith might just end up owning his own farm they both live in town while their houses are being built.

Beanstalks can grow a good height. When planting bean stocks we cut 8 foot bean poles and space them about three feet from each other, this will allow them to grow. Most people on the farm like Chaney just like to lean on the beanpoles and smoke because it makes them look cool. Getting a good wrap around the pole is important too. I think all and all my father Mr. Henry has planted every kind of crop you can think of from orange groves in Florida to wheat in New York, he has been everywhere a farmer can go. Mid-west to east back to upper Midwest, my father is a true down to earth farmer. He travels to the farmers market show every year to show his prize winning cabbage. This year Dad decided to grow the largest melon, he plants a special patch and keeps all of us away from them, no matter what the fruit or vegetable is Mr. Henry can grow it. My father does this every year. He begins by setting up his white picket fence then he meshes and tarps his little projects so no one can see what he is planting. After he meshes and tarps the area, Dad usually over waters his prize crops and keeps every little bit of moister you can think of locked into the area.

~Chapter 12~
Going into Town

Going to Town

Going into town is a big deal to me traveling with Chaney, Chip, Susan, Mom, and Dad makes it an adventure every time. Mom likes to leave early in the morning especially when we go to Nashville to see Uncle Nick. When one thinks about all of the sights in town, Main Street, and the city life becomes much more interesting than the country life on the farm. Too many gun fighters and gamblers live in Nashville Tennessee this makes for an interesting area with forts that can be seen from miles around the city, we have gotten used to the area and the way people act here.

Dad came in the door "we are going into town," he announced. Mom had us packing our stuff for almost immediately after Dad had made his announcement. Packing mostly consists of us asking Mom,

"do I need this or will I need that,"

Susan and Mom were the worst at it, wondering what they should pack for Poly and I. Telling them "all I need is myself and the clothes that I have got on my back and that is it." People that need a whole lot of stuff to wear are mostly homebodies; they do not need to be doing a whole lot of traveling because those like being able to stay at home. Here comes Chaney, "Hey throw this in with you alls stuff." Susan put Chaney's stuff in with hers because Chaney never did pack anything much. Every time he went to town, he would spend the time hanging with troublemakers and staying with what Mom called hussies. Women like Chaney and it showed, Chaney could down a Royal flush in poker and double down black jack twenty-one, plus tell you the top card before the dealer throws out the hand. Occasionally, Dad would leave for town and take Chaney with him this is the type of stuff Chip and Chaney looked forward too. Chip just started courting nice young woman named Betty that worked at the Knoxville Hospital. They see each other every weekend. He travels over to her family's house and pops in for spell. This was not a good time for Chip to be leaving to go to Uncle Nick's house. Chip looks like the all-time farmer, clean-cut like a military man. Smiles and grins from ear to ear with the cool no style hair that sat on top of his head like a perfect blond wig it only needed trimming. Dad liked to wrestle around with the big boy until his hair stood on end like a badger then they would call it quits.

Well, any way we left the house on Saturday morning missing the market and church was always a big deal to Susan because this was when she got to see her friends from school and all around the neighborhood. Dad woke me up early. I got into my overalls and he told me to get the pants and shirt set on just in case he can get a deal with one them new Polaroid guys and take family pictures. I had a friend Hazel at school that had taken one and she stayed home for a whole week because the flash injured her eye. She had to wear a patch the next week, did it look ugly. The boys called her pirate all month long until the patch came off in two years one eye was blue and the other one was brown never could figure it out, Susan said that girl Hazel lost that eye but she sure took a nice picture.

Mr. Riley agreed to take care of our farm while we were away. At least for a day or two he had the run of the farm being like one of the family, the one thing I never understood was why Mr. Riley's wife Theresa did not like to come on the farm much. Mom would take something over just about once every month but she kept to herself. Mr. Riley was as my Father put it an old fart that did it the right way and that is the only way he ever knew how to do it. His wife looked no older than Mom or Susan they liked hanging with Theresa any time they could but she was a homebody too many people around did not know Mr. Riley was married. Well to make it short Mr. Riley would watch after things for my Dad whenever we went out to town. Early in the morning on Saturday, I came downstairs Chip and Susan had already started loading the big tent wagon getting it ready for travel.

"Give me that stuff,"

Chaney said, "Well come on with it" he barked a second time. He was outside already arguing with Chip about how to organize the bags. It was not much stuff; Chip had started to load the bags in the middle of the wagon under the fishing net Grandpa had brought us from his traveling sales job. He must have had the net for a long time because it looked used by the time it showed up here, the net already had holes it. Mom said, thank you and it came from Granddad so no one said anything about it being over used before it got here; as the net hung in our tool barn on top off the sycamore tree grove hill we never really used it for anything. "You will see everything will fit in the middle," Chip waved his hands to explain to Chaney. The two bench seats on the sides were open with a little bit of space for feet to sit, Chaney shook his head and started to push more stuff in the middle of the wagon. "There everything fits" Chaney said while taking the credit from Chip. I already knew that Mom was going to sit up front with Dad. Susan, Poly, and I were going to be squished in the rear between the upper tent area next to the driver and the rear cart while Chaney and Chip sat at the very rear lift gate area. Mom and Dad liked to go over Uncle Nick's house to help him with his cobbler shop in town. He lived close to Nashville and we all could ride into town whenever we wanted to see sites.

This time we actually traveled to Nashville to see my little cousins' Aunt Sara and Uncle Nick. Last time it was to get the buggy wheel fixed. The buggy sat in the rear of the yard under a tarp, Dad did not like riding it around much because every time he did we all had to get dressed up. The buggy was much more elegant than the tent wagon. It had less space and we all had to sit with our legs crossed to fit inside of it. Madam may I have your hand well much obliged throwing your suit coat on the ground when Susan or Mom would enter or leave the buggy it was tradition that Dad and Chip had to wear the chauffer cover to make every one look important. We had to change clothes just to go out and play. Uncle Nick would rather see the buggy than the tent wagon any day, it made him feel as if someone important was in town and then he could take off from work and the people would leave him alone when they see the expensive buggy outside his house. Uncle Nick referred to the tent wagon as a roach coach because you took the tent off and it looked like a big cart on wheels that the people sold their house goods off of. Dad was not going to wear the driver cap and the monkey suit this time, it had tails and everything Mom made sure that the one driver's suit of Dads stayed clean.

It started to rain as the wet droplets of rain came down we all piled in the back of the wagon Dad and Mom sat up front they put the front cover up and we were on our way Poly cried because she said she did not like feeling wet as the rain came down on the horse drown carriage. A little rain would glide in from the rear and the front of the carriage. Mom and Dad took the brunt of the rain as we started down the road Dad stopped at our second barn and we all got out waiting out the rain that is the difference between the buggy and the wagon is that the buggy has a roof; doors and windows; on the wagon, you just had a tent.

Dad would have kept riding on in the rain but Susan and Mom complained Chip, Chaney, and I stayed quiet. Dad had a disappointed look on his face because he likes to keep on time. He would look at the windup timepiece that he kept in sync with the grandfather clock in the upstairs hall. It was brought at the market the inside of the timepiece said Eastern Train Depot on the back of it and Richard Van Bronzeswick in the inside of the casing. Well he sounded like an important man hope nothing happened to him to lose such a nice watch. Dad always said,

"if I run into him I will give him back his time, a man with a wealthy name like that needs to have a timepiece like this."

As the rain started to let up Chip was playing with Poly's bonnet and she would laugh because he made it look like a little puppet with a mouth. Mom did not mind as long as he put it back on but it irritated Dad because he thought he would be late plus Dad did not like them teasing little Miss. "You boys stop playing with her bonnet and get these packages on the back of the wagon better situated. Dad wished he did not say that. When the rain stopped and we were ready to go Chip and Chaney were still messing around with the luggage and Mom laughed any time Dad got frustrated with the boys he would put them to work and this time it back fired on him. Dad hopped into the back of the wagon looking like a thief with the twisted mustache from the rain and a blank look on his face they rustled around inside then Dad jumped out after all of the packages where in the back perfectly. Mom gave Poly to Susan. Susan put Poly's bonnet on and we all jumped in the wagon in the same order as before Poly, Susan, and me at the front of the bench, Chip and Chaney in the rear looking out of the wagon tent. Dad kept his shotgun just in case something happened on the way; Chip and Chaney both have shot guns. They each have two but Dad told them to leave them inside the house. Instead Chaney carried his little pirate pistol, it was not a rifle, you could only shoot it once and then you have to reload it. This added extra security but Dad was the only one who really needed to have a weapon in the bunch and Uncle Nick had a whole case of weapons if any one needed them but Chip acted too civilized to ever need to protect himself that way.

As we rode the bumpy road to Nashville, we saw several people selling apples with their fancy little stands they had them lined on the connecting horse trails. Going the opposite way from Knoxville to Virginia, you could run into Indians. Dad took the fun out of the stories because they move along the trail looking at you the same way you look at them. They have something to sell you but my Father liked to only deal with business partners. Chaney was more of the type to be out there and win himself a squall. The trail to Nashville got dark at night that is the reason why Dad liked to leave at the break of dawn, when we took out the day was just beginning and now looking through the leaves of mid-July you could see farms and homes, and one or two church chapels. Dad liked to trot through the roads his horse map showed Anderson Creek trail and we followed it right down to Uncle Nick's house. When we got to Uncle Nicks our cousins Lou Ann and William came running out Uncle Nick was at work and Aunt Sara was out back at the creek making a wash. Dad unleashed the horses and had Chaney walk them to the stable for water. Lou Ann said, "we were expecting you earlier Uncle Henry and Aunt Rebecca. Dad reached into his pocket pulled a handkerchief out and then dug further as if he had something to give them. He yelped at Chip bring them candy boxes around Chip came running around the corner with two little dyed canisters full of wrapped saltwater toffee

"Here, you two go", he handed them a piece or two of the candy and then took the rest inside and put it on the counter. Dad stormed out the backdoor and down to the creek to talk to his sister in law Sara. Hope we are not intruding on yawl city folk nothing but houses on this side; they had some yard an acre across. Susan and Poly stayed in the same room, Mom and Dad in the living area. Chaney and Chip stayed in the guest shack or out in the tent wagon. They liked to camp out, it made them feel like men in the wild. Chaney making forest noises and Chip making carnival noises sounding like a safari they both

136

sounded like wolves in the night. I went out to say good night to my brothers and I could hear them from afar "hey Chip get them stinkers out of my face" and then Chip laughing at Chaney. When I got closer and saw the two camped out in the tent wagon it made me feel left out of the fun just lying under the stars and eating a pot of beans and deer jerky makes it a good day. Dad made it clear that he wanted Poly, Susan, Mom and I to leave Chaney and Chip alone and let them have their fun.

I said my good night, Chaney and Chip gave me the go to bed and I took off to the house. As I was entering the door Uncle Nick was packing a new pair of shoes and asked what I was up so late for, Nodding "I needed to use the outhouse" he said "just use the bathroom upstairs, it has running water and all." I proceeded to my room closed the door and went to sleep on the floor next to Williams bed. The next morning my cousins Lou Ann, and William were getting ready for school, they went to school all summer long Susan and I do not go to school during the summer. Chip and Chaney had already left to help work with Uncle Nick in Nashville and Aunt Sara was in the kitchen with Mom talking about the new knits that they had. Mom went on about a new dragon fly loop she learned from a young Indian girl in Knoxville. Poly just ran toward me then she would plop down on her pamper tie, she did the same thing three times before she got to me. William uttered to me, "you can go to school in my place today Christopher, I will stay home on vacation." "No, I do not think Dad or Uncle Nick would allow it," I responded. They both took off out the door and they walked fast to school. While walking to school they played through the ball Lou Ann did not look right throwing a ball in her study dress she did it anyway. Uncle Nick and Aunt Sara did not have many chores to do around the house, they had a self-flushing toilet and running water all of the stuff went into a tank and they used a pump to pump it out every month by hooking a big fire hose to it that run out into the forest behind the house.

Dad always said it was unsanitary but Mom liked having the toilet inside the house and not outside. I sat on the couch, looked through some books, and found an adventure book called William Clark and Lewis Mid-West Adventures. Therefore, I sat and read about a guy who was an explorer as he got chased by the biggest bear in the world and survive to tell about it. Then he hikes throw geysers of steaming water and enters an area where the buffalo ran wild and the trees grew gigantic. After sitting at home and seeing Poly run out and in the kitchen over and over again, to see if I was still in the sitting room. I ran outside to find someone to play with; if there were any one to play with, I would have found them. It looked like a bunch of women walking around gossiping about their women things that had nothing to do with me. Running out to the creek like the wind slashing through the trail when I got there, I pulled a string from my long johns and made a pole out of a fallen branch whip. Out of the branch and tangle from my long johns I made a cat fishing rode to be exact, I took a bent nail and looped it with doubled string turning the nail into a hook. Plop in the water it went one, two, three, four, five six, seven, eight, nine, ten, eleven and to fifty-eight then something bit and the branch curled over, it looked like a little perch. As I put it back in and looked at the subtle water for a good thirty minutes or so I landed a cat fish pulled it in and wrapped it in my shirt. After ten more minutes I landed another one and at about fifty minutes I had three cat fish wrapped in my shirt. Started my way back across the field to head home just my over-alls showing skin and wrapped fish, when I got in Mom looked surprised.

Now look at that little fisherman, better get up stairs and change your stinky self and stay away from those fish. Leave them in the kitchen Mom yelped, and I moved as she had a change of heart. When Chip and Chaney got back they hooked tiered from helping Uncle Nick or chasing little women around that's what Susan said as soon as they entered the room. Guess who Chip and Chaney new friends are. Mom told them,

"stop that gossip and go down to the stream and catch some catfish for dinner"

she held up the Three I caught and they sobbed as they got the fishing gear from Uncle Nicks stash. Chip picked up a net and a pole and Chaney grabbed a hook a rope and another fishing pole. Then Chaney through one to me, "come on fish boy we got to work for dinner." Susan went on telling Mom about the two girls that came in the shop, tried on shoes for two hours, and then said they would be back tomorrow. Mom, "That is what they did they came in and looked around they only liked the help did not really worry about the shoes." Chip laughed as we all walked out the door Susan had her pink slippers in her hand as we all walked out. Walking down the trail you could hear the trickling of the water as if someone was pouring it from a pitcher. "Hey, you" Chip said, "No, do not fish by yourself Chris; you can never catch enough fish to feed a whole family it takes three or four people with you to make a meal." I told Chip," I was board and needed to do something three little fish are not enough I know, just did not want to throw them back." Mom decided to have fish because the ones I caught looked good. About this time, we were next to the creek bed and we could see a crayfish move toward us, "Hey Chaney get the bucket send nature boy here to go get it" Chip said. Now I was running back to get a bucket. I ran to the back of the house, grabbed the tin bucket, I ran back. When I had gotten back, Chaney said, "not bad for a fisherman without a boat got me two in only ten minutes." Chip had one he took the net and scooped up four crayfish, "this is how us manly men get fish and provide for our family." I caught another one but it was too big for me to reel in so Chaney took my rod. He pulled the big black ugly catfish in and stuck it in the net that was hanging in the stream. The net was held up by a big rock that Chip and Chaney had moved on top of the pole. Chaney decided to take his boots off and put his feet in the water. Chip pointed and said," get your hairy feet out of the water, when the hook gets you better not blame me." Then Chip started to make ape sound," hoo hoo aha aha aa aha ohhh oahh!" Chaney put his rod on the bank and started making the same sound," ohh hooa aa ahooo aoaa ohhh!" Then I started to drag around a big limb scratching my head like an ape and Chip put his fishing rod down and started chasing Chaney. Chaney ran behind a tree and throw grass clumps at Chip while they both made ape sounds Whooo ahaaa oohhaaa woooh aaaah!!! I ran over and threw the branch into the water and Chaney ran toward Chip with his hands under his armpit saying, "whooo hoooo hooo." Chip let out a large,

"Whoo hoo aaaaaaa."

Then they both met up with their backs bent over dragging their knuckles on the soft dark colored mud next to the creek. As they approached each other Chip grabbed Chaney around the head as soon as Chip tried to put Chaney into a choke hold, Chaney ducked his chin and moved his head from side to side to break lose. Then they were wrestling on the ground until Chip came up on top Chip, had about thirty four pound on Chaney plus he was the older one then they laughed at each other and we all went back to fishing. We caught five more fish two perch and three big catfish. "Hey lets go home it is starting to get dark," that was the way Chaney said we were done. "No, Chaney we need to catch about five more fish," Chip said. "OK, let us move down to that deep area over there" Chaney responded. We went over to the deep area and waited for fifteen minutes before catching anything else the sun was going down and we were hungry from being out fishing. I could see Dad walking over the grass area in front of the sun, a pail man with a hairy beard and straight mustache with straight eyebrows to go along with them, he started to yell from a distance come on in and eat dinner. Chip had to say what?

He came closer, "You boys pack it up and come on in to dinner." Chaney just reeled another one in stuck it in the net while Dad turned around and headed back toward the house. Chip looked down and said I thought this was dinner, we grabber the bucket of crayfish, the net, and hook full of fish then started through the path back to Uncle Nicks and Aunt Sara's house. When we had gotten in Mom and Aunt Sara had the food on the griddle ready to eat. Dad sat down with his face stern when Uncle Nick, William, and Lou Ann came in the kitchen, his face lightened up like a candle that almost went out but stayed lit with a little bit of wax. I had not seen Susan all day except for when she came home from the shoe store. She sat down then Poly came running in "I am hungry," Poly said, "I am hungry ," then she sat up in the high chair looking around after a while Mom came out with chicken and rice and we all ate smelling like fish. Chip kept pulling on his shirt color because he must have been itchy from all the work he did today. Chaney tried not to make fun of Chip looking down at his food. We said the grace, then all the sudden out it came and it came from Susan why not change your shirt you look like you are jail bait and got caught by the collar. Everyone had to laugh and then silence and Uncle Nick said, "Yes I guess I worked the boys and ladies pretty hard today." Seeing the fish in the wash bucket plus we all smelled like fish Dad said," after you all finish dinner get washed up," yes Dad we all replied. Uncle Nick added his in to and said," William and Lou Ann you best just not follow." After dinner, Mom and Aunt Sara both stayed behind to clean up the fish, got packed, and sent to the outside icebox. We all went out to the horse barn to get washed up as Uncle Nick poured the water in the catch. Susan and Lou Ann headed upstairs to the washroom. We could only shower two at a time. William and I went first as Chip and Chaney pumped the stream water after Uncle Nick showed them how to do it, "See pull on this cord then you push in and out this pump."

Then Chip and Chaney went next as William and I pumped the water. After we had finished washing and changed William, I went inside, and Chip and Chaney stayed out in the horse wagon. As we went inside Chip and Chaney were throwing beans into a hot pot. Mom and Dad had gone to bed and Susan, Lou Ann and Aunt Sara were knitting in the fire room, while Uncle Nick read his paper from this morning. William had some books to read so he handed me one and we both sat on the floor by the kitchen breeze way and read for a while. Uncle Nick had fixed up the playroom for Mom and Dad to sleep in and I stayed in Williams' room while Lou Ann and Susan shared a room and Poly stayed in the guest room across from Mom and Dad some night's Mom or Dad would sleep in the room with Poly.

I finally went to sleep after reading about a man who built a steam cart and how newly elected president Lincoln was going to make these steam engines for the whole country. William said you going to school tomorrow I said, "no, my parents want me to stay around the house while we are visiting." "Oh," William said and he pulled his covers over his head then all I could see were his night cloths poking out from the back I rolled over on my mat and went to sleep. William usually walked up the hallway to use the washroom every night and during the day none of us are able to get in there with Mom, Aunt Sara, Lou Ann, and Susan getting dressed running in and out of that room for no reason at all. The next morning it was dark outside like the sun did not want to show its self the old man had not gotten up yet. It was four o'clock in the morning, I went out to check the eggs and get morning milk the rest were steady cleaning up and Chip and Chaney had slipped some clothes on to go to work with Uncle Nick.

Chip was using the outhouse and Chaney was watering the woods when I looked over. Chaney yelped out, "you got about thirty minutes before you two have to be awake." I looked over my shoulder and heard Chaney's voice from a crack in the outhouse door. William was right behind me he was still in his sleep clothes following behind trying to catch up and help us with a couple of the morning chores. It always helped me to get started early in the morning. William and I went into the chicken coop, grabbed a dozen eggs, and milked the cow for about two gallons of milk. They have three cows out there and four horses. We then went inside and gave the goods to our Moms to cook breakfast for us. Susan said, "What you could not get more milk today." I responded, "That is all I was told to get." "all right" Susan said. Call Chaney and Chip to get two ice blocks for the fish, milk and eggs. I ran outside to see that Chip and Chaney were already in business suites, "Susan needs you two to get two Ice blocks for the in-house ice room," they took the red planting wagon over into the Ice section of the barn and brought two square five by five blocks of Ice out. The ice was delivered once every two days. I could see the wet marks on Chaney's suite when they had finish Mom got Poly, Lou Ann came in the kitchen and we all sat to eat breakfast. Mom sat down and watched Uncle Nick and Dad share a newspaper that Uncle Nick had got from town, the Tennessee Journal it had all the information you needed to know. Then both men hiding behind papers looked like two spies trying to send each other information in secrete. The paper would fold and you would see a mustached man take a swig of juice or get a bit of eggs and then the paper would go back up. Poly was sitting at the edge of the baby stole that Aunt Sara had in the kitchen. Chaney liked looking out the windows like a getaway man and Chip well,

Chip was just Chip. William and Lou Ann had a proper domineer about them. They sat with their little napkin in their lap and arms under the table until they needed to eat. Even when they sat on the bench in the fire room they sat with their leg straight up and down like the play dolls sat. William and Lou Ann both crossed their legs and placed both hands in their laps as if they were praying at the table.

Dad tried to say grace whenever he could remember too but lately everyone has been running to the table so we say it individually for the time being like last Saturday Dad told Chip to speak up. You could hear him across two rooms when he says it, "Well speak up boy! Say your grace!" Then Chip would mutter out some words of praise that sounds like a preacher trying to waste time at the end of church when his notes ran out. After wards we all say God bless and eat. Uncle Nick then put his paper down and started into his morning prayer mumbling God is good, God is giving, thank you lord for this gracious living, God is mercy, God is grace, Thank you lord for this here breakfast plate. God Bless. Then Mom went over to feed Poly and every one dug into their food. There was no pass me this and that at breakfast this happens when everyone has to go someplace important Uncle Nick slurped his boll of porridge down, the egg muffin sandwich went away from his plate like a magic trick.

Chaney and Chip did the same thing and Dad asked Uncle Nick if he needed him to help out at the shop today Uncle Nick said," I think Susan, Chip and Chaney are enough but if you want come out for a day be my guess." Therefore, Dad ran back to his room to get his good shirt and tie for the shop by the time he came down stares Chip and Chaney were almost out the door. Uncle Nick had his four person cart outside ready to go Dad looked and told Chaney, "ride low" Chaney moved to the back squatted down like a gunner on the back of the open buggy holding onto the left rear chair. As they rode away, I waved good-bye and Dad, Uncle Nick and Susan waved back. Uncle Nick juggled the horse straps as if he were running late for an important appointment. William and Lou Ann dashed out the door and took up the street moving their feet fast before long they turned the corner and no longer could be seen. Mom and Aunt Sara stayed inside all day long.

Therefore, I went out to the Barn area to see what I could do today. All of the children went to school in this town there just is not anything to do around here. I went and feed the four horses that were in the barn and changed the water out. Then sat and looked on as the sun set over the dense trees in the area just outside of town. I saw Uncle Nick's next door neighbors briefly they looked like a bunch of people just making it by. Uncle Nick did not have enough land to do nothing with; my guess is that they all worked in town or on the new railway that President Lincoln was building through every major city. This paid well five cents a day to be a layman. Too many people are traveling up north in search of the good life. Granddad said it is not a pick nick in the New York area. People are tough up there and you need to protect yourself. More and more immigrants are unloading themselves at the docks and the sick increase every day from malnourished travelers to Ellis Island. I was board and went to the barn to mess around. My Uncle Nick had a big climbing rope that lead to the upper shaft of the barn; I climbed up the rope to the top portion of the barn. He had a rope instead of a hay lift. When I got to the top of the barn the rope tied to a big crank and under the rope at the bottom was a square cut out that could be cranked up and down as needed, pretty neat contraction for a none farmer. When I had reached the top it was dark up there, I could look through the rafters and see sleeping bats at the other end of the barn. I must have scared the ones off that sleep on the end when I climbed up on to the deck. I remember seeing the same bats at night circling the orchard trees in the back of Uncle Nick's house. Looking down at the ground the darkness stopped me from exploring up in the loft of the Barn any further.

There was a candle up in the loft next to a nearby rail; there was no way to light the candle without a candle lighter. Mom came in with her black dress and white work bonnet on looked around after making a lull spin. Looking like a spindle she whorled around "Where is that boy she said out laud to herself. Then yelled," Christopher" in her monotone voice. I laughed my laughter gave me away, she then looked up into the loft, shot to where the rope was, then I poked my head down with one hand on the edge of the flooring and the other on the rope Mom said, "doing all right" I said, "yes maim" then Mom said," Lunch will be ready in an hour." I forgot that I was the only man at the house that day, "yes Mom" I responded and then Mom left. After Mom left, I started to mess around with a pitchfork that one of my cousins had left in the loft. It is funny, if you put a work glove on the handle end of the pitchfork then jump on the other end how far away will the work glove fly in the air. Aunt Sara must have gotten tired of sowing this type of glove. I have seen the cow leather type of glove all over the house and when we find a left glove without a right glove, we just fold the left one inside out. I climbed down the rope and ran to the outhouse by the tented wagon Chip and Chaney were staying in and then sat outside in the heat. When I first entered the outhouse, it smelled but it is cooler inside the outhouse than outside. After being inside the outhouse for a while, the smell went away, but the outhouse seemed to become hotter. I grabbed a piece of the daily newspaper from last week that Dad or Uncle Nick must have left. It was located in a basket hanging on the wall of the outhouse. After wiping clean then I used the wash bucket to clean my hands and proceeded inside to see what Mom had for lunch.

~Chapter 13~
Building Two Guest Houses

Building Two Guest Houses

It was Sunday and we had just gotten home from church when Dad decided that he needed a guesthouse to facilitate his new employees Bill and Doug. So what he did was place an order for lumber by Jack Ripple in town he had Chip and Chaney run the order to Knoxville then Jack Ripple sends the carriages to the house for unloading. They only knew one way to build a house, it was the traditional Two Decker Tennessee farmhouse three rooms upstairs with a bathroom, and five rooms down stares with a kitchen, living space, play room, dinning, and study. Dad hired two new workers to manage the farm and needed some place for them live. This is the kind of stuff we do during the winter months when crops are slow only the orchards produced product and everything else was small product like green beans, spices, hot peppers, and tobacco. These fields only grew with a lot of attention during the wintertime. We had to tarp the small areas to make sure that frost did not destroy them.

We were all in school when the shipment came down Sycamore Street heading to our farm Dad had ordered a full two knuck of wood to build the houses. Miss Parity could see the four large pull carts go down the street as a circus had just come to town. They pulled just about every type of wood you could think of. Dad always did things on a large scale nothing was small to him. When the carts came rolling down the street Miss Parity stopped her study and asked,

"Children whose parents are building today?" It was just Susan and I, Chaney stayed at home waiting for the lumber come in. Susan said, "My Dad is building two new houses on his property for the new workers and their families to live in while they manage the farm." Little Mike Thrash said, "I would rather go help them build than stay in school all day, building is a trade." Miss Parity looked Mike over and told him, "Without math skills you cannot build a house, a builder must be well educated to measure the pieces in order to make then fit properly after they are cut."

Mike sat down and did not say another word. Mary and my sister sat next to one another during class and wrote messages back and forth all day. Peter was a year younger than me he was eight I am nine so I sat a row behind Peter and every once in a while I would pass a funny picture to Peter. We are so close to the teacher that we have to be very secretive to pass notes in the same manner my sister Susan and Mary did. Miss Parity asked," "Do you and Susan need to leave school early to help your father with his building project." "Susan blurted out," Chaney is at home with my other brother Chip my father Mr. Henry and his three workers that should make for enough people to start in on building the house." We only had two hours left in school and I was ready to go home in order to see what they had planned on doing with the building materials for the houses. Instead, I kept my mouth shut nodding along with what Susan had said, then I turned the page in my grammar book to study for the end of the week spelling test. It is important to get every word right on the spelling test this keeps you from having to study on the weekend and having to take the test again on Monday. We studied grammar for the last two hours of class. Then Miss

Parity went out and rang the bell for the end of the day. I grabbed my stuff that I had left in the cubby area. Peter's father built the cubby about three months ago. It made it easier to gather your stuff when you have your own cubby hole to put your lose items in. The new coat rack made it easy to grab your coat and hat for after school. All of us waited for one another at the big oak tree. Susan, Mary, Peter, Sandra, Clair, and I all walked home together. Peter had to stop in to drop off his books and then he caught up to me. Clair, Mary, and Susan had kept walking and I was walking slowly waiting for Peter to come back out. Peter's sister Sandra went inside Peter told his Mom that he was going over to my house and then he caught up. We walked down the road until we saw the construction wood carts that sat a little off the roadway.

Jack Ripples name is written large on the side of the construction cart it said Jack Ripple Lumber and Building Corporation. I did not expect Mr. Ripple just to leave the lumber inside the big carts but that is what he did. He must have trusted Dad with returning the cans. Dad and every one were out moving all of the lumber form the cart to the shelter that Chaney, Dad and Mr. Riley must have built earlier. Peter and I just sat and watched we were of no use to them at all. Dad tried to make us look busy by tells us to pick up little things on the ground. Then he asked Peter and me to get his work supplies and nails from the barn. We both ran off and grabbed some of the large digging shovels, then brought them over on a cart leaving the cart next to the work shed. After about three hours the sun was going down and they, Dad told everyone to stop unloading the wood. There were only two wood carts left to unload, the men had unloaded the other two. The rest of the work would have to wait until tomorrow. We all went inside where Mom, Susan, Rebecca and Juliana had food on for all of us. Peter stayed for dinner and we ate soup, with wild turkey Dad had every one gathered as if it was thanksgiving or something we ate in the dining area of the house. Mr. Riley's wife came over with bread and cakes she set them in the sitting room Bill and Doug's wives helped Mom cook and serve. Chaney invited his girlfriend Clair over. She made a pot of tea and some juice. We all ate and then after eating Bill and Doug began the journey back into town to where they stayed for now. Peter got a ride from my Dad and left to go home. I waited for the cart to pull up then hoped in it to ride up the street to Peter's house. Dad dropped Peter off in front of his house waved at Mr. Peters who was on the front porch and took back out of the dark area then we went down the hill to go home. When I had gotten home, it was late and I was sleepy. I ran out to the well to get some water to clean my face and then went inside passing the barn Dad was putting the horses into the stable for the night. They had their own running in the pen and stable. I went upstairs to bed preparing for the tomorrow.

After doing, my daily chores having woken up at 4:30 am, feeding the horses, and cows cleaning around the pig pin and chicken coop I then fetched water for breakfast. Susan was up getting something ready in the kitchen her and Mom must have had some kind of agreement with preparing meals. "Hey Susan, need some water?" No but you can get a fresh pail of milk. See Chaney always told me to keep my mouth shut when passing the kitchen area; this is one of the times I wish I had listened to Chaney. I went out to the barn and picked the one cow that did not do make a hassle when I milked her. She was a black spotted white cow that Dad never did like but kept around because she had very good milk; she was about 2 months along. After getting the milk, I went inside to see everyone sitting at the table ready to eat breakfast. I plopped down in my usual spot as I could barely see Dads head behind the newspaper, he then put the newspaper down when Mom passed by after setting Poly in the high chair. Mom knocked the paper with her finger making a popping sound that made Chip who looked tired from yesterday jump in his seat. Susan laughed and said," "Not much on noise today." Chip looked up and smiled saying nothing. Dad said," "Is he dead in the grass while hunting." About this time, Chaney entered the kitchen. Dad said, "Rebecca could shoot better than we did, the deer knew to run when ever Chip let off a jump just like he did at the table. "I got my eye on him," Chaney said. Then they stopped the improper talk because Mom started to lean over the table. It got quiet for a second and then Dad started to say grace.

Please and forgive, help us, then a pause study, and then gracious food amen, this was all I heard while looking out the window at Mr. Riley pace back and forth on the porch. Right after Dads legacy grace, we started to pass around the bread and eat the eggs, sausage and drink milk. As we sat and ate Doug, Bill and Mr. Riley were all standing outside getting ready to do some work. Mom finished eating quickly and cooked up some grits, eggs and sausage for the guys outside, "Chris and Susan could you take the nice gentlemen some of the food plates." I finished up and Susan had a half egg to go before she was done I went ahead of Susan and took two plates of food out to the front so the guys could eat.

Out the door I went, Blue howled a little as if he had not been feed. Blue eats off every other plate any of the away. Pompom was nowhere to be found he liked to hang around the sheep pen. When I had gotten outside the fellows were standing around talking, much obliged tell Mrs. Henry thank you for the grit, they started eating immediately after we brought the food out then Susan came out with orange juice and muffins.

Chip came walking up and I could see Chaney stretching his back from a distance, Dad was trying to keep an even space between the houses on the road. Mr. Riley came up and asked where should they start digging? He had two oxen and a large pull shovel they needed to dig a twelve-foot indenture into the ground before starting to build. Dad told Mr. Riley to start about two acres away from our house he measured it off and began to even the area that Dad pointed at by moving the push shovel over it. The other house was going across the street with a little path leading up to it just like ours. After three hours or so, the carts that had the wood on them where completely empty, the six men had cleared the wood and I could see Doug's head while he was handling a pike axe. Chaney had a shovel and Bill and Mr. Riley cleared the dirt with the horse cart and two mules. It seemed like they had only been working for an hour.

Before I knew it, Mom was bringing lunch out. "Christopher, go inside and grave the two pitchers of lemonade for us please," Mom said while juggling a couple of plates of food. I went inside found the two steel pitchers of lemonade sitting on top of the closed barrel. Steadily with fast feet, I brought the pitchers of lemonade out to the men. Mom had Susan bring the rest of the food out. Susan carried thin sliced meet

and sandwich fixings to feed the men for lunch. Chip
was the first one over, "What do you have here." The
wind blew all day as if to say I am going to keep my
hard workers cool. The other two, Bill and Doug's
wives had just showed. They left the carriage on the
road and came down to help Mom. Dad had Chaney
park the carriage by the barn after the women went
inside to help Mom. They were inside making salad,
pruning vegetables for dinner. Dad called lunchtime
and everyone gathered around the table. We ate
inside. After lunch, Chaney and I played with the ball
in the field. Doug really was not good at catching; he
stuck a sock on and started to through around the ball
with us. I noticed that the rain was coming, the clouds
were dark and the wind was picking up. Dad told
everyone to bring it inside. Chaney and I ran inside to
see Poly, Mom, Susan, plus Bills and Doug's wives all
sitting in the living area talking over tea. We all got our
food digested while Dad, Mr. Riley, Bill and Doug
gathered the tarps. Dad stuck his head inside are not
you boys going to help us tarp the work area. We put
on our rain galoshes and ran outside to work with Dad
and crew to get the area trapped. Right as we left out
the door Dad and Mr. Riley already had two large
tarps on the horse wagon heading towards the big pit
they had dug. Chip and I were out at the barn trying to
fold our tarps on to the cart, "Hear hand me the corner
short stuff" "Chip said. With a smile, I handed him the
tarp corner and he yanked it on to the cart as the
dusty tarp went over my head I pushed up in to it
throwing the bundled part of the far end of the tarp
onto the cart. "Look out a big throw from a little guy
this is a franchise game of rugby," Chip uttered. I
looked up at the rain coming down in bigger and
bigger droplets, hopping in the front of the cart as

Chip yawed it on the horses began to move slowly. Entering the digging area, there was deep mud. Dad and Mr. Riley already had half of the pit covered with their tarps and then we pulled ours off the cart and started toward the dug area. When I put my boot in, it sank about three feet this meant the pit had already been dug to about three feet down. Chip yelled, "Get out the way little stuff." Chaney was waved over, "What do you need," Chaney said. Chip responded, "Put this tarp over that dark mud spot right there." I struggled to get out of the way, then sat on the edge of the pit and pulled up just enough that my boots did not get stuck in the mud. Chaney came my way gave me a hand and pulled me up out of the mud, while I stood next to the side of the pitted area. Then Chip and Chaney grabbed both tarps and pulled them over the mud area. Usually Dad would work straight through the rain but this rain was harder than usual. After tarping, the dug area Dad told us to go in the barn and change over. That is exactly what we did, we went into the barn and got into our clothes bin, changed up and were ready to tackle any obstacle that came.

Mom came outside to get clean, as we ran inside from the barn and sat in the study, Mr. Riley left to go home at the same time Bill and Doug started on their way to town with their wives. Dad told Doug; hold up the hotel for the day or at least until the rain stops. Chip, Chaney, Susan and Poly all stayed in the playroom while Dad and Mom talked in the kitchen, Dad speaking, "We need to get both houses up by the end of next month, before the cold starts to sits in." Mom responded, "You may not want to rush the building of a house it could make the house build worse than if you took your time Henry." "Rebecca,"

Dad answered, "with the kind of help we have these two houses should be a cinch to put up just a little elbow grease and hard work." I saw Dad sit down in the old chair and Mom handed Dad a cup of fresh coffee. I was listening in from the other room when Chaney hit me in the head with a stuffed bear. "Aw, why did you do that," then I turned around to throw a little satchel at Chaney, "OK big stuff," Chaney wheezed out. Walking to the door and out on the front porch where you could see the rain droplets coming down drowning the plans for a quick easy building day.

When I came back in Chip was laid out on the floor reading out load about George Washington cutting down an apple tree. When George Washington was to cut the tree, he went out with an axe and chopped it down for firewood to provide for his mother, this came about before the Revolutionary War. The book had George Washington portrayed in a Minuteman's suit and we all knew that George Washington was a General and Generals are a higher rank than a Minuteman is. They portrayed George Washington as starting as a regular solder. I grabbed the Mother Goose Nursery Rhymes book and started to read out load just like my brother. Mixing up the nursery rhymes, I said," with a twiddle Twiddle dom Jack heart his thumb, sent Jill to fetch a pail of rum When Jill fell down jack was not around she turned the bucket into a crown." Chip laughed because he said, "that is not the way the nursery rhyme goes, read it right Christopher." Poly thought it was pretty good she laughed and grabbed a toy block. I started into saying another nursery rhyme correctly, when I came back in the door Dad was in the kitchen wondering who just left out the door and let the cold air in.

Dad yelled across the rooms breaking Moms no yelling clause, no yelling or screaming inside the house

"Close the Door,"

Dad said in loud voice! I went and shut the door and then Dad got in trouble with Mom who was making marmalade on the pantry table. "No yelling in the house Henry."Yes maim," Dad said with a smirk. It all sounded like mumbling from outside but I knew what happened because it happens every other night when the fall nights get cold no one wants to bring in fire wood and coal so they yell when the door stays open too long. Then Mom gets to have her civilized talk with whoever yells first. It helps to stay snug underneath a blanket. The cold comes in from that front door and then moves to the side pantry. No one even uses the rear deck because our dining table blocks the door. Dad likes to do things his way and his way is to put the dining table next to the rear door with a chair right in front of it.

Chip said that Dad is keeping the rear porch clean for when he decides to make it the front of the house and change the whole house around. This will never happen Dad keeps the rear pouch unused this way, the deck will never sink in. After playing around with the nursery rhymes for about an hour, I decided to start reading them correctly. Little Miss Muppet sat on a tuffet, Eating curds and whey, along came a spider and sat down beside her and frightened Miss Muffet away. Hickory Dickory Dock, The Mouse Ran up the clock, the clock struck one and the mouse came down Hickory Dickory Dock. Little boy blue come blow your horn, the sheep's in the meadow the cows in the corn,

Where is the little Boy who looks after the sheep he is under the haystack fast asleep. After reading a couple more of the nursery rhymes, I started to fall asleep Poly lay on the floor and Chip left upstairs to carve his wooden model. Susan came down and started to knit some new hand warmers.

Mom was steady in the kitchen preparing supper a big pot of beef stew, she was cutting carrots, Dad went to his bedroom and Chaney must have left out to the barn loft. It was two hours later when Susan started collecting us up for supper. We all sat quite as the rain poured down and you could hear the roof tin making tingling sounds. Dad, Chip, and Chaney had big plans for the day but Mother Nature had other plans that must be more important than ours. I sipped down my soupy stew, well that is the way I liked to eat mine everyone else had more meat than vegetables. I liked to use the spoon to sip down the broth; this made me look more dignified at the table. I could tell it bothered Chaney because he did not like anything repetitive, seeing me pick up a spoon full of soup, blow on it, then balance it into my mouth made Chaney get irritated. Dad did not mind very much. Poly tried to do the same thing with her meat and it even bothered Chaney more when he saw Poly pick up a little piece of stew meat, blow on it, then drop it, and tried it again. It was impossible for Poly to get the meat to stay on her baby spoon. Chaney looked down at his food without lifting his head, woofed it down and excused himself from the table. Then you could see him out on the porch with the rain coming down feeding the dogs.

Poly finally got tired of picking up each piece of meat and decided to use her hands, Chip with a grin on his face, smiley boy finished and excused himself.

Then left out the door to meet up with Chaney to have their older brother pow wow. Susan started to help Poly with her food while Dad finished off his food he uttered a couple of words, Christopher help clear the table and get the kitchen ready for the night," this is what I got for being the slowest eater. Yes Pa" and I continued to the sip down my stew while Mom looked pleased with the dignified eating habit I had. The cold started to settle in and it was old man winter knocking at the door.

See everything we do has something to do with the holidays and the weather. The way I think is that first, you have Easter this is the time for cleaning and getting ready for the next crops. We wear our suites to church and dress up for town. Then before you know, it is June. In July, we have the first harvest and the second planting of the season. On July 4th every one lights fireworks and goes to the carnival. August, September, October, Halloween is the time to start winding down and get repairs done on the house. This year Chip and Chaney made scarecrows for the farm and a hayride for all of us with little ghost stories for each area we passed. This was fun we did it every year Dad needed to see what we could come up with. All of the workers, Mr. Riley, and our friends came out on Halloween to enjoy themselves with a little fun some apple cider, a mule ride, and a maze that Chip and Chaney put together every year. Thanksgiving is the time for having people over and hanging out to eat up all the leftovers from the summer months. Every other year Grandpa or Uncle Owen would stop in and visit. Uncle Nick came over every year and my two cousins from Nashville William and Lou Ann traveled with Uncle Nick and Aunt Sara. This is a very exciting season for me because we get time off from school to visit with relatives and Christmas is just around the corner. Christmas is a time for giving, each of us get to make something for everyone else. Last year, I helped Mom make candles to give away to friends, we always have something going on interesting during the Christmas season. It makes it fun to open gifts that everyone has taken time to make all year around.

Well it was late when I had finished my soup, I picked up the rest of the table that Mom, Susan had started to clean, and I grabbed a couple of plates and stuck them inside the dish bucket. After wards cleaning the table, as Susan complained about how Chip left mud under the table. "You eat too slow Christopher if you were like Chip and Chaney you could have been out playing but no you have to do things the Christopher way." I said, "At least I do not slurp when I eat." "Kudos to you," Susan said as she went into the kitchen. Mom came in and told me to straighten the table. "Could you please straighten the table Christopher," yes Mom I responded and then they both started to wash the dishes by using the bucket of water and the wash tube. Each time Susan washed a dish Mom would rinse it with a splash from the bucket.

When I had finished straightening the table, I then went into the game room to sit and look out the window at the splashing water droplets that were coming down. It made a puddle outside and the ducks were out there playing in it. It was a round circular puddle, as each droplet came down the water rippled as if the droplet of water was making space for more water. The ducks seemed not to mind as they squawked in the puddles and quaked at each other taking large strides and flapping their wings to cruise over areas of mud I noticed the webbed feet and how the rain did not affect the way they lived. The deer hid under the trees when rain came down the only other animals that do well in the rain are frogs, turtles, and fish but fish are under water. My estimate is thin fish do not count for dealing with rain. At this time, I got tired and went upstairs to go to bed.

The next morning, I woke up early and got myself dressed with some overalls. After getting dressed, I then went out to do my morning chores cleaned the chicken coop then milked the cow and fetched water for breakfast. Chaney had to feed the cows, oxen, horses, and the chickens. Chips job is to clean the outhouse and burn the dung. After chore time we washed up and went inside where Susan and Mom had breakfast waiting for us to eat. Chip and Chaney had nothing to say all morning long they just ran around the farm.

Chaney had graduated from high school last month and he was now staying home only going to school occasionally to help as a teacher aid. Chaney received his graduation note from Miss Parity our schoolteacher and put it behind glass. This meant no more school for my brother now he stayed home with Mom and Dad all day helping on the farm. Clair Chaney's girlfriend is a year younger than Chaney is, he would walk her to and back from school some days of the week.

Hey, "dodo head pass the jam," as we all sat at the table this was the way Chip liked to ask for things. "Say please" I said. Susan passed the butter glob over to Chip so he could butter his bread. "Thank you little sis," he said while Chaney still looked like he was just waking up in the morning with blood shoot red eyes. We saw a big yawn come out of Chaney then

Dad said," tired from yesterday huh." We all nodded our heads and then started to eat. The eggs where sunny side up today, Susan liked to overcook some days of the week, the porridge from Mom was just good enough to stick to the stomach all day long. When Susan cooked, she liked to make eggs, grits, and pancakes. We ate pancakes for breakfast, lunch, and dinner. They would make them out of potato Doug that really made the pancakes tasted good. Dad liked putting tomatoes on his like a sandwich we all ate the potato cakes like a pancake. Tomatoes made it too runny for me.

Clair was outside and you could see her head poke in and out of the door. Susan told her come in but Clair was one of those who ate like a rabbit. She ate little to nothing and stayed the same size as Susan who eats all day long. We did not judge her for it, but the only meal she would eat is dinner, all during the day Clair ate nothing but toast. "Well invite her in," Mom sounded flustered.

Chaney excused himself "Excuse me every one," Chaney said in his mannerist voice and then he headed towards the door to talk to his girlfriend. Chip laughed and said, she always comes over when Chaney is getting ready to do something." Dad looked over his paper and said, they will get their timing together." I stayed quite while pushing the ball of the yoke across my plate because the fork would not pick it up. Thinking to myself, I should have done it Moms way and scooped the whole egg up then placed it on a jelly toast. Daybreak came slow today most everyone had their selves ready for school early. Bill and Doug came in they were ready to work today. "Hey little stuff go and tell your Dad that we are here" Bill said. I went and got Dad, he came in the room and said his good morning making fun of their unwashed faces because you have to go to the parlor every day to get a good washing in the city. "Need some water for your stick em," Dad offered Bill and Doug to the well. He was not too worried about them being cleaned up. Dad asked Mom to put two eggs on and some coffee. Mom went out to the chicken coop to get eggs we all slipped out the door Susan, Clair, Chaney, and I while walking up the street we meet up with Peter and Sandra.

Peter's father had started on building a train to town from his property, too many people wanted to hop a ride from Mr. Peter. It was made for the transport of his harps; he had started to put together a couple of cars. Mr. Peter had to rustle up the money to buy him a turnaround track; I think that is what he called it. This new train was making Peters back yard like grand central station. As we walked to school, Chaney asked Peter, "Peter is your Dad going to open his train to the public or what is he going to do with such a machine." Peter responded, "If he does, you will be the first to hear about it." His train was in the local and national newspaper and people were traveling far and wide to see his train move down the track.

As we approached the schoolyard, Mary ran up and handed out brooms, Peter and I grabbed a pail to start picking up fetch. Chaney pointed some junk out on the ground then turned said good-bye to his girlfriend and left. Miss Parity came out and rang the bell; we all rushed in and sat down. Miss Parity started in on our homework assignments making math out of household items. Curtis a new kid spoke about his grandfather clock. Curtis explaining, "My grandfather is what I did my math assignment on. If you see an XII this is twelve o'clock, and a III is Three o'clock VI is six o'clock and IX is nine o'clock this is the way we tell time in my house." Everyone clapped and then it was Susan's turn to do a math problem from the house. "I did mine with the feeding of a cow and horses if each horse takes one-pitch fork of hay and each cow takes two pitch forks of hay how much hay would you need for eight horses and five cows." As she explained, Susan wrote the problem on the black board. She showed the eight horses across from the eight pitchforks of hay and the five cows across from the ten pitchforks of hay all together, Susan went on, "you would need eighteen pitchforks of hay." Everyone clapped and Miss Parity went into how wheels move. She explained, "think of a wheel as a pie each section represents a piece. If you have a pie cut into four pieces and three are eaten how many pieces will you have left?" One piece everyone responded so what percentage is this one piece.

This is where Miss Parity lost me. I did not understand what she wrote on the board but it looked like this 4/4 and ¼ then ¾, this was the type of math Dad did. A while went by then Susan looked and said it was a fraction. This type of work seemed to be for college but I have seen Dad and Mr. Peter write this way on building items and leave it there on the wood that they wrote it on. Percentages seem to be a good way of getting out of counting the actual merchandise. As Miss Parity went on to explain she drew a big pyramid then added that the higher area is less than the lower area. This meant the lower part of the pyramid was more common than the higher part of the pyramid. Then Miss Parity lost me completely when she went to explain," if you were to be excellent in the class, where in the pyramid would you want to be" Miss Parity asked. Mary raised her hand and blurted out, why at the bottom because more people are at the lower half of the pyramid. I know better than to be at the bottom.

Mary messed up, Miss Parity's whole discussion went to the crapper in a flash. Miss Parity responded, "You were supposed to feel special to be in the higher area of the pyramid." Miss Parity continued, "There are less people in higher area. This means that you are among the elite being in the top of the triangle." Mary did not see it this way the top looked to her like below average because it was smaller than the bottom. Miss Parity then turned the triangle upside down explaining, "This is what you see everyone at the top and less at the bottom this could happen to you if everybody does well in the class." Mary was right it was important to make the area that most people can fit in at the top and the ones that are unable to accomplish to a minimum.

After our discussion it was lunchtime Miss Parity had Percy ring the bell and we all let out to eat our bread and cheese. Susan, Peter, Mary and I liked to eat fast so we could talk to friends that we do not normally see. Sometimes it is nice to talk to David and Marshal my brothers' friends even though they are older children. I do not like playing with the younger children they all like to play on the little kids bars. Some of the lessons are made for the older children and not the younger. Then other lessons are for the younger children and not the older. I heard of them changing the classes around so younger children met one day and the older on another day but Miss Parity insisted that learning was learning and that there is no difference between age just understanding. After we ate Mary started talking about the new train station that Mr. Peter was working on with the City Officials. We still had war going on around the area a couple of odd scrimmages were posted in the towns newspaper last week that made people around our way very unsettling because too many southerners started to have undecided values toward the North and South.

Many family men moved out of Knoxville before their family life was mixed into the war. The Forts where not the safest places to be around. Fort Sanders in down town Knoxville was a place of siege but the town seemed to still, operate around the fighting. I moved on to sit by the oak tree with the children my age. I am only nine years old and I am not interested in the Civil War, the only thing I really knew about it is that it took my friend William away; he used to hang out in Knox while we sold food. William a nice guy about my age, him and his father decided to join the confederate army and I have not seen them since. My Uncle Owen is always writing letters to my Dad and Mom he tells them about conquests thin they go on and how well the United States Army is doing in battle. While sitting under the tree Sandra came over and sat next to me Peter liked acting like the older children so he stayed over with Susan and Mary.

"What are you doing Christopher," I responded, "Looking to see if Frank will fall off the swing set while he swings upside down."
Sandra looked over at Frank's goofy ways and laughed at him. Now I have seen the smaller children play on the swings and fall off, but Frank seemed to like to run, and then jump into the swing set, laid out on his stomach then Frank would swing. The rest of the children liked playing marbles, jumping rope, dodge ball, and hopscotch. I am always it; I liked to play tag for some one that is slow like me. Sandra

looked, saw an open spot in the jump rope line, and then took off. I went to see who was taking whose marbles today the older children controlled this game and I was not in today. Then Rick Rang the bell and we all ran inside. I slide into my chair next to Bill and Peter in front of Mary and Rhonda, Clair sat in the very back of the classroom and Sandra sat at the end of the row with Rick, Mary and, Joseph. Chaney's friend Marlin was always sitting in the back of the class with Clair and one of the five Mary's. Miss Parity started into proper grammar and pronunciation of Subject and Verb. What is a Subject? Miss Parity asked Mike, he did not raise his hand but he was called upon to answer the question for some odd reason. Mike was not wearing his school clothes and Miss Parity noticed it and called on him for an answer. Mike went on mumbling something out even though he did not know the answer it went like this, "A subject is an act that someone is performing in a book sand a verb is the area of the subject." See he was kind of right but did not quit get it, Miss Parity told everyone, "give a hand to Mike for his try" after clapping Miss Parity pulled down on her spectacles and then blurted out the Oxford Book of Grammar definition for Subject and Verb. Miss Parity went on to explain, "A subject is a helper word to a Verb that represents a person place or thing.

A subject is what the sentence or paragraph is about the verb is who, where or the place the sentence is explaining about." This all confused me as Miss Parity went into it a little further we all started to copy down notes just in case we need to know this information latter. Before I knew it the bell rang and we were out of class. Clair's younger brother David was waiting outside and her older brother Bradley with Chaney, Susan, Sandra, Peter, Ricky and I all started to walk down the hill. It seemed as if Clair's brothers came out to help my Dad build. Mr. and Mrs. Hancock had been over and it looked promising, Dad would get help if he requested it or not this is just what families do in the south they really liked Chip, Susan and Chaney and you could tell Clair's father wanted Chaney as part of his family. Dad has the type that never left a debt undone but when someone volunteers their family out to help, one might want to take their kind jester and use it.

It started me thinking about when Chip and Chaney were going to build their houses Dad had land plots down the street for them that way they had their own space to farm. Just right after the school there was woods down at the bottom of the hill this twenty-two acres Dad bought was for Chip and Chaney to live and farm. Rick lived down the street about ten minutes further. Peter asked if I wanted to see his father's train my Dad had talked to Peter's dad about letting him use the train to haul some goods to town this way my father could open a grocery store right in Knoxville. While we all walked home from school Rick kicked an old little rock with his shoe as it skidded around the dirt road Peter or I would stop the rock under our shoe then kick it again. Chaney, Clair, Bradley and David had made it further down the road. Dad was still working on the houses you could see two skeletons of houses one across from the other standing as if they had to fight to stay in their place.

Dad only liked building a traditional two-level farmhouse with a wraparound porch for sitting items ready for sale on, this is where Mom spent most of her time sowing in the rocking chair folding cloths and churning butter. Of course, we helped Mom with all the chores and Susan and her friend Mary liked to hang around with Mom while she went through her daily routine. Peter and Sandra's house came up first and I stopped by to see how the train was doing. This time Mr. Peter had a log cabin with a large over-sized deck that had items that needed to be shipped to town, the actual train was behind the shops in town and Peter's father was shipping from his distillery every day. After seeing all of the progress that Mr. Peter had made we proceeded down to my father's project of the houses being built and helped gather nails for Dad, Chip, Chaney, Bill, and Doug. "Hey look its four eyes and his accomplish," Chip said while swinging from the top of the roof with a rope like a monkey. They had beams in place and tied a couple of ropes so all they had to do is climb up and then tie the rope around their waist and push off to move to another area to place finishing nails in the siding.

Mr. Riley was not sure about this method he liked to use the ladder only he would move a large rock to put behind his ladder, every time he would move it you could see Mr. Riley hunched over the large rock. Then while moving the rock Mr. Riley would hold his back where he wore his leather brace. "Oh lordy lord," Mr. Riley would yelp every time he would move the ladder and then the rock, but he never asked anyone to help him move it around. Mom liked to see Dad run around the half-built houses with his hammer and work belt made of gun holster that Granddad had left one Christmas. Chaney hit the nail once or twice and it was in, he made few mistakes here and there putting a nail in the mistake, he completed more than both Bill and Doug put together. Chaney went across the street and worked on the second house with Bill and Doug while Dad, Mr. Riley and Chip worked on the first one closer to our place. Peter's Dad came on horse and buggy," where is your father at."

I pointed over to the other side of the house then Peter and I ran behind the buggy wheels to where my father was. Mr. Peters stopped right where the corner of the house ended and yelped to father, "Hey, Henry." My father poked his head out of a window with no pain and Mr. Peters handed Peter the rope to tie the horses down. While Peter tied the horses to a stake in the ground, I made my way over by my father. Dad said jokingly, "Hay is for horses." Both laughing Mr. Peters said, "fine houses you got here thinking about making house building a business. Dad responded, "got two families of workers living in the City, you know the town is not safe at night; they need a protective place for their family. I will give up a little property for them their wives and family. "Mr. Peter responded," Why such a kind hart Mr. Smith, well to do what we can." "Christopher told me you might want to move some of your stock to a storefront in town," Mr. Peter explained to Dad. Dad responded, "Yes sir, now how would you propose to make that happen," Mr. Peters waving his hands explains," well if we get track laid out right down the creek way, you can make staging area that I can pick up your stock. If you need additional train cars you gotta build them yourself or get Mr.

Orval to give you a build price and we can extend my little train further down the road if you want a shop in town." Now-they were planning a grand train station in town that could carry people up and down the coast what Mr. Peters was doing was getting a move on early before anyone else got a claim. Dad then shook Mr. Peters hand and then Mr. Peter told Peter to get in the cart ,"Peter come on let us get home for dinner, they both waved good bye as Mr. Peters took of turning left then right to the road as they disappeared. Just before sun down Dad called it quitting time and we all headed inside to wash and get ready for dinner. When we got inside, I noticed that Clair had helped Mom and Susan with dinner but Clair herself was just leaving out the door with Chaney as soon as we got inside. Clair's two brothers Bradley and David came over to help with building the houses then around dinnertime they left to get washed up. Chaney's spot at the table is up for grabs some days during the week. This way we knew that Chaney and Clair had become a thing.

Mom was the secretive one she always veered away from trouble, Mom liked the Hancock's and tried to help them out every opportunity she could. Mom and Susan had set up the table and Chip was the first one to open his mouth about Chaney," Looks like we lost one." Susan laughed as Mom sighed ever so slightly, Dad looked back and forth as if Chaney had ran out the door without a trace Bill and Doug had already ventured to the city they must have been happy because it was their last week's stay in the city of Knoxville no more worry about being caught up in war. It seemed that they did not like the night travel so as soon dusk came they both went back to Knoxville them and their wives rode together home an hour or so after lunch. The funny thing was that Poly ended up in Chaney's seat so the table did not look too empty. It was the Hancock's turn to share time with Chaney who they all liked any of the away. Susan put the mashed potatoes out and gravy. Then the ham soup with vegetables soon came out and a large loaf of bread. Dad must have been tired of reading his newspaper over and again because he did not have the newspaper in his hand at dinnertime.

Dad left his pipe next to the door Mom passed around hot tea and lemonade. The fire in the kitchen stove kept the house warm. Chip sopping up soup with the bread did not have much to say blurting out, "I think we need to add a third house to our building." Dad looked around and said, "Yes Chaney has grown fond of Clair Hancock and he may want to marry next year if all works out right." See marriage in my family went pretty fast six-month courting, two months engagement, then you are married after eight months. This happened to be my Grandpa's rule he liked to see the marriage no matter who it is in the family go his way. "Would you clear the land for Chaney," Mom asked Dad. It will have to be right after Christmas and then we have got to work fast? Mom wanted Chaney and Chip closer to the house and the workers to live further out, this does not leave Chip and Chaney very much space to farm for themselves. "Face it Rebecca both of the boys are of age to live on their own," Dad said as he looked over at Mom then to Chip. After a brief quietness, Susan started to collect the dishes up. Mom stared me down as if I was doing something wrong. Then in a blink of an eye, I was with Susan picking up dishes. Chip excused himself and went outside to test his new pipe out. I had only seen him smoking cigarettes but today he stepped up to a pipe. It was dark and you could hear an owl who hoot through the chilled air. It was not exactly cold but it was cool for fall. About this time in November, my Father liked to sell at the Gallery but we had so many projects going on that the Gallery had to wait until next week. Tomorrow Susan and I had to go to school. I went back inside after using the outhouse and sat inside the living area to watch the fire burn in the fireplace. While Mom and Susan canned goods for the market, Dad went out to the porch to talk to Chip.

You could briefly hear Dads large voice over Chips semi large voice talking about what they thought about the houses being built. Poly came into the room with her Miss Nancy doll and sat looking at the sparkle and crackle of the fire as it charred the log in the middle barely touching the ends. Susan had made some cookies for us to eat and brought them into the room. I was full from dinner but there is always room for cookies. After eating two cookies my belly stuck out of my good pants, sending Poly off to see Mom with a cookie in her hand, I ran upstairs to get ready for bed. When I got up stairs, I put on my red long johns and tucked under the sheets in the cold room I figured that Mom, Susan, and Poly would probably sleep next to the fire down stairs tonight.

~Chapter 14~
Finishing the Houses

Finishing the Houses

I woke up early, it was still dark and the time had already been set back on my alarm clock. I set my alarm clock last week. It was 4:30 am and dark. I was up ready for chores before school. Chaney happened to be up with the feedbag on his prize horse Sundance. Susan is usually up getting Marcy ready but today she was still asleep by the burned out fire. While I was feeding the chickens Chaney walked pass with a piece of wood "early bird gets the worms," he said I nodded as Chaney dropped his hand and went into the house with the new log. It was still chilly and you could see your breath as you blew out. After feeding the chickens and milking the cows for morning milk, I went inside with two pitchers of milk and a basket of oranges that had been left in the barn from sales the other week. Mom came down and said, "Well look at how good of worker Christopher is," I smiled and Mom went into the kitchen to do her thing. Chip just peeped his head in the door and then went back outside. I went out to the barn to wash and change into my school clothes.

When I came inside Mom had breakfast ready, some ham and eggs from the icehouse outside. We sat and ate as the two, Doug and Bill arrived from town. They sat in the living room and ate at the same time. Their wives had not arrived yet but today was the finishing day for both houses. Mr. Riley usually showed up around 7 o'clock am. He likes to eat at home with his wife Mrs. Riley who is better known as Theresa. She had become a good friend of the family, since she is mute, we could understand her head nodes she was a proficient writer we could read notes from Mrs. Riley all day long this is the only way to communicate with Mrs. Riley. Mrs. Riley sends some homemade biscuits or bread for us to eat every other week. Dad liked to keep close to his employees and listen to their issues and problems he especially liked the ones that attended church on the weekends and had their own families. He always said, "a good person is worth a thousand words." I think this analogy came from Granddad's analogy," A bad person is not worth spit." My father made it sound more civilized his way being positive and all. Clair came in and Chaney excused himself from the table, "Excuse me my honey beckons me." With a glass of orange juice in front of Chaney Susan pored him another glass and he looked down as if to say what is this for, Susan shooed Chaney away saying, "it is for Clair, being early in the morning." As Chaney and Clair sat on the porch out front, Bill and Doug were talking about how nice it was going to be to get out of town because they had random gunfights there Bill was telling his story of how they had to make a getaway last month.

Bill explained, I was outside the Grand when two fellows came by wearing South. The Confederate tried to enter the hotel, the keeper told them they were not welcome. Why not they asked? The one stranger looked over then a patrol from the North saw the Confederate suite from across the street, He then proceeded to see what was going on. About this time guns started to be drawn, I kept my revolver in the holster in the back of my belt. The minute I saw them start to wrestle, a shoot went off and the North patrol went down then the two Confederates moved their weapons on me. I started to put my hands up as the left raised one raised the right hand caught hold of the revolver and bang down went one across the street. Another North shot the other and I ran inside to escape for my life. This happened when Bill first moved into town and no one ever did believe his story. He would have had people all over looking for him if he had gunned a soldier whether North or South. Everyone liked to hear Bill's story. Dad said, "Tomorrow you will be able to move in and have your own place to stay in this will keep you from being involved in to much nonsense with the civil war." They expected if a battle had broken out near town that everyone would help but our area was too undecided. The funny thing was that they are predominantly for the Union especially because Vice President Johnson is from Tennessee.

There were stories of husbands and wives that disagreed because of where their family was stationed at and the fact that the further South they lived the more cutthroat they got toward the Union Army. We tended to our own since it seemed that the Confederate was not going to stand up in the end no one wanted to fight for a losing force, they wanted to all be winners. I finished my food collected up the dishes and went into the living area to say high to Mr. Bill and Mr. Doug. "Look at little Chris he's beginning to look like his old man more and more every day," Mr. Doug said. Mr. Bill laughed, "Now you got book learning all around your farm this is going to be a successful business for us," Mr. Bill said while patting me on my head. Got your books Christopher "yes Dad," I answered, "Go on and get to before you become late," Dad said. He threw me an apple, "give this to Miss Parity," "OK Dad" I waved and went out the door where I saw Susan, Chaney, and Clair already by the field post. Then I got to running and caught up with them about mid hill towards Peter's house. Chaney liked to jump up on the empty tree limbs and swing around; he was just a big show off for Clair. Clair told him to get down before he gets himself hurt.

"Get down," Clair said, "that branch could break and then you will be in the sick bed."
Susan and I were already used to seeing Chaney clown around on the trees he never fell, Chaney and Chip could climb the highest trees and stay in them all day long. You would walk under a big spruce and they would send a pinecone dropping on your head. This made me not like walking under trees because you never knew when one of them was in it. Chaney climbed down and then we proceeded past Peter and Sandra's house they were both up the road by the time we passed their house they were almost at the school. Susan started to walk faster and I was in the middle of Susan and Chaney. Clair was in the back.
Then we saw Rick come running up from nowhere huffing and puffing to get up the hill, he had been running. He caught up and said," "Boy, I thought I was late." We still had fifteen minutes to make it to school. Carrying that apple in my bag made the side of the bag poke out and it looked like a big knot. "What you got rope in your bag?" Rick asked I looked down and pulled the apple out," it is for Mss Parity from my Dad." It helped to give something to the teacher this way my father knew that he would always be the first person to get the scoop. When we had got to the school it was full of children cleaning, they dusted, swept, and picked up the outside like normal. Today, I ran into Rhonda she was running out the door with a

broom and I was coming in the door to put my bag up when thump we both ran into each other while the door jam held the front door Rhonda and I fell down the front step. Her knee in my chest, it hurt but I did not cry. We both got up fast looked around to see if any one saw us then dusted our selves off and went back to cleaning. Miss Parity came in the back door brushed herself off, as the minute she entered the door it started raining a cold fall rain that freshened the air. Not equipped with a raincoat we all ran inside and sat down as the rainstorm got worst. Miss Parity asked did anyone hear about hurricane seven that was headed this way we all nodded no because our parents did not go into town every day.

Miss Parity liked to receive a paper every day but you have to ride into town about thirty minutes away on horseback or one hour fifteen minute on foot. Since Miss Parity had a coachman take her from and to town every day, it would not surprise me if she had a newspaper with a report in it. The Atlantic coast fishery report from North Carolina posted in the Knox News says that today and tomorrow we will be hit by trenching rains that will not end until Monday afternoon. OK my father definitely has bad luck when he chooses to build a house. Mary fell over in her chair then caught herself just before she fell asleep. Miss Parity did not even notice it. After about ten minutes she were in to Hurricanes in depth asking first, can anyone explain what a hurricane is" We all raised our hands but little Thomas Mackie sitting up front got his hand up before Peter. I was somewhat wishy washy about a response.

Little Thomas said Well it is a sort of storm that moves up the coast very fast with scary winds" The older children had to laugh because the scary winds sounded funny. Miss Parity even smiled for a second, then she said he is kind of right. Hurricanes move up the east coast usually between September and November it actually moves seawater to the land. Then makes it rain on the land with high enough winds they blow up to one hundred miles per hour. A hurricane is able to force a well-built house out to sea but since we are so far inland it only lets out rain and about fifty mile per hour winds that is not as bad as the Carolinas get. Then Miss Parity went on by pulling out her barometer, and explaining, "the first one was made in 1643." What is this machine and what does it do? I was the only one with my hand up, "Yes Christopher." "It is a basometer and it measures the pressure around us." None of them laughed except for Miss Parity she smiled, "very good Christopher but the name of it is a barometer, again invented in 1643 by Evangelista Torricelli, he worked with great astronomer Galileo," Miss Parity explained in detail. Miss Parity passed the barometer around the class as she explained, "the mercury core of the barometer detects lows and highs of the atmospheric pressure that turns the needle upward on the barometer as it reads atmospheric pressure.

This atmospheric pressure can predict a rainstorm or hurricane by comparing past reading from other years." The only one I had ever seen hung at Granddads old house and it had a big ship at the top of it with three dials and a compose under the ship that rocked back and forth when it was uneven to the ground. After passing around the barometer, we then took a break as the wind started to pick up a bunch of the students parents were already at the schoolhouse to pick their children up. My Dad was outside with the rest of them it really must be bad outside. Miss Parity brought a couple of things inside and then dismissed class. I thought it was funny to go home because of a rainstorm but from what Miss Parity said, this was no regular rainstorm. Susan, Clair, Rick and I all hoped into Dads cart and took off down the road. While all the rest of the children got into their parents wagons and left the wind had picked up and it was whistling around the trees. After a couple minutes of fast winds, it started to down pour harder and harder. It felt like a man with barrels was pouring water down on us when you looked out the rain came down and the air looked like shaken sheets. The horses started to panic on the way down the hill and before we knew it, we were home. Chaney and Chip were at the new farmhouse across the street Dad went into the one up the block to put finishing touches on it with Doug and Bill Mr. Riley was across helping work on it with Chaney and Chip. It did not matter to the men the fact it was down pouring rain they still stayed in the house and finished it. Dad had the pipes coming tomorrow after piping the house with water he was going dig two new wells. Get your selves some outhouses built by the end of next week for these two houses and you will be doing just fine Dad told Doug and Bill. The rain came down hard and did not let up at all I could see a little red man running back in forth that was the color of my Dad's rain jacket that he had gotten while working with the local Fire Department as a volunteer. Bill and Doug looked like little gray people as they held their hats and walked across the mud. I looked out the study room window and saw some of the hardest workers I had ever seen. Repeating the old pony express song Mom said, "they work weather rain, snow or shine," She said this while passing to the kitchen mom put a pail out the door to catch some fresh water to stew with. Susan was upstairs she had Poly and was changing into some clean clothes that were dry I figured that if I stayed next to the fire that my clothes would eventually dry out. Mom caught me the next time she passed looking for Poly and said, "Christopher go upstairs and change out of those wet clothes before you catch cold." "Yes Maim," I left up stairs to get some clean clothes out of my clothes bin. After getting dressed I then ran down stairs where it was just becoming an hour before noon Mom had soup on for everyone when I had gotten back down stairs you could see Chip and Chaney standing next to the door with their rain trenched clothes and rain coats in hand talking under the porch.

If we continue to work today, tomorrow both houses will be done. After they had dug into the land lowered the mortar and stone placed the roof supports, and made the trusts the side walls and roof went up easy as one, two, three. Then they built a second roof for the immediate second floor that only keeps water from damaging the porch Mr. Riley was in the barn working on the porches all they have to do is put the porch in place and the houses are complete. Dad, Doug and Bill all came up and they shook off their boots and went into the living room where I was sitting, Susan placed some couch covers over the ones that were there so everyone could sit down. Hey Henry, "where was he when you needed him huh," "he was out at school they let them all come home early because of the bad weather." "We never got a day off from farming because of weather there is always something to do every day in this industry." Doug said, "How much did you learn in school today?" Then I told them, "Miss Parity taught us about the barometer today." "What is that," Doug said. Dad looked over and said, "you do not know what a barometer is?" Doug said, "No." I went on, "It is an instrument that tells the atmospheric press." Bill interrupted, "OK *layman* terms it tells us when it is going to rain or not." Mom brought in some chicken soup and bread so we ate and talked. Mr. Riley came in from the barn and Susan handed him a bowl "thank you kind miss" Mr. Riley said, then he started into Chip, "As slow as you work we are lucky to be done." Dad laughed because Chip and Chaney had never built a house before especially a two story and Mr. Riley was the expert at it. Chip smiled and told Mr. Riley, "Well as long as we have got Dad and you we have no need to build any more houses."

Bill blurted out, "You have got all the know how you need Mr. Chip."

They finished eating and went back outside to work on the houses out in the terrible rain and wind. Mom got on me about not picking up my things in my room. I ran upstairs to pick up the belt and my sack off the floor. Mom, Susan, and Poly stayed down stairs next to the fire while I stayed upstairs in my cold dark room trying to clean whatever I could.

After about thirty minutes and cleaning I came down stairs to see Blue and Palm Palm sitting under the fire with Mom and Susan knitting on some quilts. "Go get your study books and read until dinner." "Yes Mom" I said and went into the study room as we could hear the rain banging against the door like someone knocking. Our porch is covered with an extended roof but the force of the wind is so great that it pushed the rain directly into the front door making a knocking sound. Dad was outside and a couple of branches where flying around in the front while the men ran in and out of the house closes to ours. I wanted to go into the barn but Mom told me not to go outside unless it is an emergency. So I stayed inside and read a comic about Dusty Landers the New Frontier Cow Boy. It went on about how he could rustle eight horses with one lasso and catch the cattle robbers with a quicksilver musket. I liked the way the illustrations were, they were vivid and colorful. My Grandpa must have left the magazine about two Christmases ago. He was always leaving something around the house, one year a wooden duck the next year, a chess and checkerboard. We liked receiving gifts, Granddad always had something to give away when no one asked for it but when you asked for something it never came that is just Granddads style.

After they had pretty much secured the two houses Bill's and Doug's wives could move into the houses as soon as the weather got better. From what Dad and Mom had discussed, it is too expensive for Doug, Bill and both their families to live in the city. In addition, the war is going on if an attack broke out, they would have to either stay and fight or stay with us, it would be too crowded in this house for two other families. After reading my book, I went into the playroom and started to play with one of Mom's puppets that she had stitched. Before long, it was dinnertime and the sun had just about fallen in-between the rain clouds and all of the wind that gusted in this late season storm it began to rain harder as it got later. Dad and everyone continued to work even though it was night time you could no longer see anyone outside they had all moved their projects into the house itself. Stair cases the stoves and wooden benches where all being customized inside the newly built houses.

Mom waited for the men to come in you could see Doug, Bill, and Mr. Riley getting ready to head home after a long days work. Dad, Chip, and Chaney all continued to work. Mom told me to sit down and eat. Susan and Poly both sat at the table eating our quit dinner because without the guys to joke around with there was not very much conversation. After eating bean stew I was getting tired of the whole eating stew every other day and wanted big man's food like steak and corn but during the wintertime that type of food was scarce. Mostly eating stews and fish during the winter and any other jar types of foods that can be stored for long periods is how we ate. Dad would bring home deer and bear for us to eat during the winter but this type of food was hard to store so he dried the deer and rabbit for jerky by salting the meat it made it last longer. When Dad, Chip, and Chaney finally came in, they made some of the bean stew. I was upstairs lying in bed and could smell the fresh air of rainwater when the front door opened and slammed. The muttering of three men as they went into the kitchen to find a pot of stew then after about ten minutes you could smell beans and ham threw the air upstairs.

~Chapter 15~
Uncle Nick Leaves Nashville

Uncle Nick Leaves Nashville

Mom and Dad called Chip and Chaney in on our family discussion when Dad announced that William and Lou Ann will be moving in with us he said, "William and Lou Ann will be saying for a couple of weeks while Uncle Nick and Aunt Sara get settled up North." We needed to clean and make space for our cousins. Uncle Nick and Aunt Sara are moving to Pittsburg where Uncle Nick can make a fresh start as a cobbler. This decision came after troops have blocked the streets in Nashville. This made it impossible for the business owners to conduct business. The condition of the Civil War made it a fast moving young man's fight that only spared the victims of innocents throughout battles that occurred in town. I knew from hearing many explosions at Fort Dickerson, it is located through the woods on the opposite side of town and Fort Huntington Smith that is parallel to Fort Dickerson. Our involvement in the Civil War was to fight in order to stand up for our own property. Too many tombstones were starting to appear where Uncle Nick lived he has had to protect his property just outside of Nashville nearing Murfreesboro. Uncle Nick was not in a safe area. Dad had told Uncle Nick to move about a year ago. Uncle Owen already handed Dad and Uncle Nick pardons from the war signed by President Lincoln for their effort, of owning personal farms in our little farming community.

This War made us independent landowners that only hired workers. Uncle Nick was going to join up with Uncle Owen in Pennsylvania; Aunt Sara was going to live with Grandpa, and his wife, while William and Lou Ann stayed at our house until Aunt Sara is settled in Pennsylvania. After the newly built Train station had been seized, living in Nashville had become a late dream for Uncle Nick who was in the face of serious danger. Dad discussed Uncle Nick's dilemma with us and was planning a way to meet with Uncle Nick. He was already on his way traveling to our house and had sent a telegram to town that he would be on his way with William and Lou Ann. The dangers of war in the South had made it hard for us to live our everyday life without fear that a battalion would not march through and take our farms away. This was not likely to happen being that we lived in a community that is about a half hours way from Knoxville.

During the whole war, we have only run into Indians and runners for generals, our Sycamore area was just too rural to be part of any major fights. Our land was spread out along the countryside. Uncle Nick had planned to help Uncle Owen because the war had ruined his business and his property had just too much fighting going on near it. Nashville is a major city generals like to take control of this city making it an award of the Civil War. Uncle Nick was wounded last year from a skirmish that took place just outside of his housing area. Dad and Chaney went out to meet up with Uncle Nick while Mom, Chip, Susan, Poly, and I stayed at home. Dad and Chaney saddle packed Sundance and May to go out looking for Uncle Nick, who must have left just about an hour ago to follow the trail to our house. When they left,

Mom was outside waving at Dad and Chaney. Poly and I played in the toy room down stairs Mom and Chip went upstairs to make an extra room out of Moms parlor in the attic. It had a window and everything the roof lowered slightly in one area.

Chip proceeded to install a wall and a door to separate the storage from the room. Some of the stuff we had up there had to go out to the barn. I stopped playing and went to run some little boxes out to the barns upper shaft racks. After cleaning for two hours, the room actually started to look decent. Mom wanted Lou Ann to stay up there with her own space and William to stay down stairs in what is now the Toy room across from the living room and the study. Therefore, we started to move the toys from the toy room into the study. This would mean each of us had our own room. "Get the dolls off the rack Christopher," Mom told me. "OK where do you want them Mom," Chip grabbed the doll and shoved me a little saying, "you should not be playing with those." I shoved Chip back and got caught by Mom she gave me the stair down then I took the doll back from Chip and placed it on the shelf in the study room. Chip went back to putting up 2 by 8 shelves in the other room to put toys on. I watched as the room transformed from a play area into a bedroom.

At first, I had my doubts because the room looked too small to have a bed and extra space in it. When the afternoon had set in the room was almost complete. Susan was upstairs adjusting the upstairs bed and placing sheets and a tent cover over the bed. Mom went into the kitchen to fix some sandwiches and tea for lunch. As I picked up the last toy off of the shelf, Mom called us in for lunch. "Come and get lunch," Mom said. Chip with his long arms pushing

Poly and me into the kitchen like a hen with her chicklets. We sat at the table while Chip muttered grace. "Lord please let Uncle Nick be safe, lead Dad and Chaney so they may find him, thank you for the workers and the farm." Then Chip said, "Amen." Poly grabbed her sandwich and started into it. Susan was already in the pantry getting the cold tea. I was eating by the time Susan got back, Susan bowed her head as if to say every one let us say grace, "You just missed the grace," Chip said. Mom said, "Next time wait for your sister." Chip threw his hands as if to say she was too slow. I did not notice that Susan was not at the table when Chip had said grace. Poly was finishing the half of the sandwich and it looked as if she did not want the other half so Susan took her plate after saying a short prayer to herself.

Mom, sat drinking tea hers was made hot. As she sipped it down Mom must not have been hungry because she did not eat at all. Mom, telling Chip,

"There must have been at lot of trouble brewing in Nashville."

"You do not know the half of it Mom," Chip blurted out. Mom looked beat she just nodded her head with half-teary eyes. Susan had no words to say as she looked down at her plate. We all knew what happens during war, trying to stay safe and out of the harm's way was wearing us thin. That when you are faced with a decision to up hold your values no matter what you did, your whole life was affected by it.

About an hour later Uncle Nick, Aunt Sara, William and Lou Ann all came in through the door. "Can you believe it Chris it is Uncle Nick," Chip said in an exited voice. Uncle Nick gave me a big hug as if everything was normal. "Look at him getting to be a well-rounded

195

little gentle man." Aunt Sara looked at Poly my my
she has grown. Dad and Chaney came in the house a
little after Uncle Nick. We made some room for
everyone. Uncle Nick noticed the two other houses
out in the pasture that belonged to Dads helpers.
Those are sure nice houses out there. Yes, just got
them built for Doug and Bill. They must be happy to
have such a nice boss that goes all out to provide
comforts. Dad said, "You can stay and help out on the
field." Uncle Nick got quit then said, "No the farm life
just is not for me, I am going to catch up with Dad and
Owen," "Yes sir" Dad responded. "Did you want us to
keep William and Lou Ann while you and Sara get
your selves settled?" "Well much-obliged brother."
Dad smiled and showed them to their sleeping area.
They all looked tired Lou Ann and William where
sitting in the kitchen with their eyes closed. Mom went
and took them to their new sleeping areas. Dad pulled
the big mat out and set it up in front of the fireplace,
Chip and I were out of a room while Uncle Nick and
Aunt Sara slept upstairs.

Author: Ron Young

About the Writer

Ron Young is a leading scholar in computer systems technology and investigation. When he was growing up, he spent time in church, community service, boy scouts, school and sports. Attending Wheaton High School playing football and running track and field graduating from

Montgomery College in 1998 after two seasons of running track and field traveling up and down the east coast with his team makes Mr. Young a well-rounded person. Moving from the rural area of Rockville to the countryside of Frederick Maryland allowed Mr. Young to be around farmers and the country alike. Mr. Young has experience with telecommunications corporations such as AT&T and Sprint testing and designing Microsoft install manuals and flow plans for enterprise computing systems and security. After working in the computer field for fourteen years thus finding a new way in, 2005 Mr. Young went on to join the Marine Corps and served overseas. While in the Marine Corps, he went on two tours to Iraq, exemplified 4 years of service acquiring a Combat award, Mandatory Mass, and the Joint Chiefs Award. With an honorable discharge in 2009, Mr. Young then became a Veteran and then attended Kaplan University where he received his Bachelors in the Science of Criminal Science.

Everybody needs a get away from the normal mundane lifestyle of routine work and happenstance. They need an outlet that leads the imagination into a different time-period. A time period that represents the difference in the lifestyle between now and the 1800's, understanding that a hundred years ago people lived much simpler lives that had various outcomes, and conclusions that represented how hard work adds to success.

We all like to recall our childhood memories and the way things used to be when we were growing up. Listening to our grandparents ramble on endlessly about how we have it easier and how they had it harder growing up than what we have it now. *Wayward Life* is a story about a boy growing up on a Tennessee farm with his family in the late 1800's. This story whispers the sound of Civil War and the beginning of the industrial revolution that made America such a great nation.

The main character, Christopher, explains the hardships and uncertainty of the small farmer. The small farming communities that emerged during the Civil War have relevance as to keeping the country going during a time of war. Christopher tells a story about what hard work ethic, good integrity, and study can do for him and his family living on an 1800 farm. Some of which *Wayward Life* displays to the reader is how the family interacts and pulls together to accomplish tasks that are invited into their day-to-day lives. *Wayward Life* also has a child's like playfulness between friends and family that most often creates a tight bond between family siblings and friends. Simplicity is the key; thus, passing knowledge from one generation to another, Christopher and his family (the Smiths) survives our changing America during a time of war and industrial revolution.

This is a fun-loving book about a boy named Christopher Smith who tells his story about the South during the late 1800's. Christopher lives on a farm located in Knoxville, Tennessee, owned by his father, Henry Smith and his mother, Rebecca Smith. His family pulls together to get the farm work done; when they are not working on chores, Christopher, his brothers, sisters, and friends find time to play. This story goes in depth about growing up on a farm and the trials that present themselves while working on a farm. Many tasks are part of the everyday life of Christopher and his family, such as selling at the market, building houses, and finding new means of transportation that is, trains, and bicycles.

They have an uncle, Nick Smith, who lives in Nashville, where they like to visit. As Christopher stays at Uncle Nick's house and plays with his cousins, he notices that keeping close to family is important. Christopher finds himself in a world of war and peace at the same time, holding on to family and school values in an uncertain South that is in the midst of abolishing slavery.

www.ingramcontent.com/pod-product-compliance
Lightning Source LLC
Chambersburg PA
CBHW020452130626
46549CB00001B/385